GHOSTS OF GREENFIELD

ALICE: THE LAST FOUNDER (BOOK 2)

JASON HAMILTON

An Argoverse Novel

www.jasonleehamilton.com

Story Hobby Media

www.storyhobbymedia.com

Cover art by Vanesa Garkova.

CONTENTS

INTRODUCTION

This book, like the one before it, was originally written as a serial, with each chapter posted as one "episode" on my website. This was a great experiment, but one I've chosen to abandon going forward.

First off, it took too long. I loved the idea of having Alice grow up in real time as we read, averaging a month of aging in between each episode. But's let's be real, you're not going to wait all that time until she grows up. So I'm going to speed things along a bit.

Alice will still grow an average of one year in-between each book. However, I plan on putting out more of these books far more frequently. These first years will consist of eight books total, though there will be many stories concerning a more grown-up Alice after that.

So if the format seems a bit odd, remember that this was once a serial, and there's usually a large jump in time between each chapter. I look forward to hearing what you thought of it! Cheers!

-Jason

CHAPTER 1

K at forgot who she was. For the briefest moment, she was just the smallest consciousness adrift in a swirling whirlpool of light. She liked the light. It was pretty. She wanted to go to it, to become one with it. To...wait.

A part of herself joined her unconsciousness. She wasn't part of the light; she was someone else. Katariina. That was her name. She was married, she thought. S....Sergio! That was his name, and there was someone else there too.

Alice!

In a rush, all her memories came flooding back just as her feet made contact with something hard. The ground. That's what it was called. The light that enveloped her faded, leaving only darkness and a harsh afterburn in her eyes. She could see nothing around her.

She still kept Alice clutched in her arms. Now she remembered. That snake, the alternate-universe version of her husband had tried to take the girl away from her. A member of a group called Argo Force had come to save them. His name was Michael. It was he that brought her to...whatever this place was.

Alice was awake in her arms, but keeping quiet for now. Kat gently hugged her daughter close as her eyes began adjusting to the world around her. It was still dark, and her vision was still fuzzy with the afterglow of the bright light still blinding her.

"S-Sergio?" she managed to say. "Are you there?"

She thought she heard footsteps nearby. "Yes, I'm here," a voice called out.

It was her husband's voice. Just the sound brought waves of relief to her troubled mind. "Where are you? I can't see anything."

"Me neither," his voice was closer now. "All I see are these afterimages."

Kat could see them too. The one blinding afterimage had faded into several spots in her vision. She...

One of the afterimages moved.

"Sergio, I'm not sure those are..."

A scream filled the night. A piercing, haunting scream that chilled Kat to the bone. It came from the image in front of her. Now that she had time to focus, she realized it wasn't an afterimage, it was a form, in the shape of a woman. It glowed like....like a ghost.

A small part of Kat's brain wanted to say that there was no such thing as ghosts, but that part was soon drowned out by other emotions...like panic.

"Kat, what's going on?" Sergio said. He sounded as scared as she felt. Kat thought she could make him out now, just a few feet to her right. She stumbled toward him. Whatever this was, they would face it together.

More screams echoed through the night, and they were

followed by more ghostly figures appearing all around them. "Kat..." Sergio's voice was higher now.

"I'm here, love." She fumbled and finally grabbed his hand. He jumped but gratefully took her hand a moment later. They stood there, hand in hand as apparitions surrounded them on all sides. They had nowhere to run, they could see nothing of their surroundings. All they saw were pale shapes in the darkness. The air chilled.

A shape moved closer, coming face to face with Sergio in a matter of seconds. Sergio yelped in fear, but that was followed by a loud scream as the ghost touched his head. Kat had never heard her husband make a sound like that, not even when he had been shot several months earlier.

Without thinking, she leapt at the apparition, driving her fist as hard as she could into its ghostly form. Her hand passed straight through it and immediately grew numb. She screamed too, as a deep cold set in. That must have been what Sergio just experienced. Her other arm kept supporting Alice while her free arm went limp.

Okay, they were in trouble. Kat knew that right away. She was having difficulty thinking straight. Hadn't Michael sent them here to get them out of trouble? What was going on?

A bright light illuminated them from one side, a warm light. Kat looked, and it seemed every apparition in the area followed her gaze.

Standing in a small clearing of trees that Kat saw from the new light, stood a man. Fire burst from the man's hands into the surrounding air. Kat looked around at the ghosts and saw that they were all looking at the newcomer.

The flames in the man's hands erupted higher into the night, and that's when the apparitions began to move. They drifted towards the fire, mesmerized like moths to a flame.

She, her husband, and daughter were forgotten as all attention focused on this man with the flaming fists.

Kat didn't know what was going on, but she recognized an opportunity when she saw it. She turned to Sergio, who was looking stunned and very pale. "Sergio, are you okay?"

"I...yes, I think so. That thing, when it touched me..."

"I felt it too. My arm." She still couldn't feel anything from that arm, though she was vaguely aware of a faint tingling coming from the tips of her fingers. Good. If feeling came back to her arm, perhaps Sergio would recover fully as well.

"Can you stand?" she asked.

"I think so."

As she helped her husband to his feet, she took a moment to look at the man with the flaming hands. She blinked as she stared into the light.

The man was taking the ghosts out one by one, throwing flame at them and causing them to disappear. His motions were fluid and precise, every movement of his arms directing fire at a new apparition. Who was this guy?

Kat tried to support her husband but couldn't with one arm dead and the other holding Alice. But Sergio seemed to be recovering faster than she was, and soon enough they were walking as fast as possible away from the place. Kat was grateful to the man who had saved them, but she also wanted to get as far away from this place as she could.

"Hold up there!" a voice called out. It was the man with the flaming hands. "Don't worry about this lot. I'm almost done, see?"

Kat hesitated. Should they really stay put after all this?

But the man was right. Only a few apparitions were left, and it wasn't long before the man made short work of them.

"I think, we should probably find out more about what

just happened," Sergio whispered to her. He was right of course. Something strange was going on, and they needed to know more. Nothing was ever simple, it seemed, when Argo Force was involved.

Cautiously, they tiptoed back to where the man stood, flames still protruding from his hands and illuminating the area. As Kat approached, she realized that the flames weren't coming directly from the man's hands, but from two nozzles that attached to an iron exosuit that he was wearing. They were just a form of flamethrower! A part of her felt relieved. At least there was an explanation for something.

"Hi there. Haven't seen you before," the man said as they approached. He had an odd accent, sounding almost like a man from an old nineteen-thirties black and white movie, like he had a wad of chewing gum constantly in the back of his throat.

"We...ah, just arrived," said Sergio.

"Well, that's just curious, very curious. We don't get new people here."

"I'm sorry but who are you? And what just happened here?" Kat asked.

The man seemed not to hear her. "And you're dressed very strangely too. Judging by your clothing and how you're all covered in dirt, plus the baby there, I'd have to say that you must be from..." He looked upward in thought. "Portland."

"We...what?" Kat momentarily forgot her questions. "What gave you that idea?"

"I'm the detective in these parts. But sorry my manners, the name is Lance, Lance Carson."

The name sounded familiar to Kat, but she put it out of her mind for now. "This might sound like a silly question, but could you tell us what day it is?

"It's Friday, January ninth," he said.

"Yes, and..um...what year?"

He narrowed his eyes at her. She thought she saw his eyes move to Alice. "Wait, could it be?"

"Please, just answer the question, and would you also tell us...where we are?"

The man, Lance, looked up from the baby to meet her eyes. "It's nineteen forty-eight. You're just outside a little town called Greenfield, California."

Kat looked at Sergio, who met her stare with wide eyes. Nineteen forty-eight! Why on Earth were they here of all places? Well, she supposed it might have been worse. Michael could have led them back to the dark ages or something. At least this way they had access to...semi-modern amenities.

"Your daughter," Lance broke the silence. "I recognize that ring on her finger. Have they sent you to help?"

Kat looked back at Lance, several pieces falling into place. "You're a member of Argo Force." It wasn't a question.

Lance nodded. "One of the third-tier of course, I don't have any superpowers. I try to make up for it though." He raised his hands to show them the nozzles sticking out of his sleeves. "So did they send you?"

"Maybe," Sergio cut in. "But we're as clueless as you. It's kind of a long story."

Lance shrugged, "I've got all night. You can follow me back into town if you'd like."

So Sergio gave him a basic rundown of what happened to them over the last year as they walked alongside their new friend. He told him about Invergence, and how they were on the run from monsters for months. He told them about Invergence capturing both of them, and how Michael, a Founder of Argo Force came to their rescue. He didn't say much about Alice, only acknowledging that Invergence wanted her for some unknown reason. Kat agreed with Sergio's choice of words. They didn't want someone they didn't fully trust yet to know that Alice was a future Founder of Argo Force.

"Crumbs, that's a story!" Lance exclaimed when Sergio finished. "Who'da thought a Founder, an actual Founder would send you here of all places! I mean, you saw the problems we have here, but it's hardly nothing I'm sure in comparison to what they deal with day to day...crumbs."

Kat was beginning to like this man, despite her trust issues that had developed over the last year. But, she remembered, there had always been good people on the road they took to get here, even if some of them suffered for it. She lost the smile that had been forming on her lips as she remembered the Evans family, who had died because of them. No matter what happened with Argo Force, she didn't think she could ever forgive them for that. No one needed to go through an experience like that, ever.

"Well I suppose you'll be looking for a place to stay tonight?" Lance continued. "Seeing as you're not from around here."

"Ah, yes," said Sergio, glancing briefly at Kat to confirm. "We'd appreciate that."

"Ha, see I know what people want." Lance seemed positively thrilled. "They tell me I'm a poor detective, but they don't see what I see!"

Kat glanced at Sergio, an amused smile on her lips. This guy was a character. Sergio faced Lance and spread his arms out in mock surrender. "You got us!" he laughed.

"Of course I do, but let's go, I don't live too far from here."

They followed him down an empty street. They had

been on a small foothill which Kat and Sergio didn't realize until they began to walk down it. Once at the base, it was only a few more blocks before they reached Lance's home. It was a small building, falling apart at the edges, but still sturdy.

Lance waved an arm at it. "It's not much, but I'll be able to put you up for a night or two. I've got a spare room where my...well, where you can sleep tonight. Sorry I don't have anything for the little one, but I'm sure we can improvise."

He led them inside, and Kat began to rethink the whole thing. The place was absolutely littered with...stuff. There were spare pieces of metal everywhere, some part of a larger gadget, others just lying around. Where there wasn't some mechanical project lying around, there were food wrappings and dirty dishes. This man clearly lived alone and didn't entertain people often.

Lance entered behind them and scratched the back of his head. "It...ah, needs some tidying up for sure, but the spare room is better." He led them to the back and opened a door for them to inspect.

Just as he said, the spare room was much nicer. It contained a queen-sized bed with a nightstand and plenty of space to get around. Kat almost felt her knees buckle, and it was only then that she realized how tired she was. She hadn't had a break in at least twenty-four hours now, though she wasn't sure how to calculate that number given the fact that they had time travelled recently.

Lance saw the expression on her face and raised one hand. "I'll let you folks settle down for the evening. We have a lot to talk about, obviously, but it can wait until morning. If you need the bathroom, it's the room right next to this one."

"Thank you, Lance," Kat said. "We really do appreciate

it." That wasn't a lie. Though Kat had yet to trust this man fully, he had saved them from...whatever those things had been on the hill. And he knew about Argo Force, which meant that at least his heart was in the right place.

Lance nodded gratefully and closed the door, leaving Kat, Sergio, and Alice alone in the room.

They slept peacefully that night, with Alice between them. The girl woke up once in the night, but after rocking her gently, Kat managed to put her to sleep again. Thoughts still clouded their dreams, but it was still perhaps the most rest either of them had received in weeks.

In the morning, they awoke to see that the sun was already high in the sky. They would have gone on sleeping if it weren't for Alice who awoke and decided now was a good time to pull on Sergio's ear and shout nonsense in it. She wasn't forming full words, other than the occasional 'mom' and 'dad' approximations, but she knew how to get attention.

Still tired, but rested enough to be getting on with the day, Kat and Sergio stood and stretched. They were still in their clothes, they didn't have anything else to change into, but they found a hot shower in the bathroom next door, which they both used with eagerness. Kat stepped out of the shower feeling like a whole new woman. She could feel the refreshing coolness as her wet skin met the air. It was a good start to a good day, even if she still had to wear the same clothes for a while longer.

"Now then," Lance said after they had prepared themselves and gathered around the kitchen table to eat breakfast. "We have to go about establishing your identities, see. We'll need a good story."

"I'm not even sure we plan on staying in this town," Kat

said, turning to Sergio as she spoke. "We've had...some bad experiences staying in one place for too long."

Sergio swallowed the bite he had just taken, "That's true, but I get the feeling that we're meant to do something here. I don't think Michael just randomly chose this place and time. Besides, the technology is far inferior here so it will be much harder for Invergence to track us down, especially in a small town like this."

"Wait, what are you calling inferior?" Lance said, taken aback.

"Uh...actually the stuff you have here looks pretty advanced," Sergio responded. "You're a gifted mechanical engineer."

Lance puffed out his chest. "You make a good deduction, son! It's a powerful hobby of mine."

Son? Lance was no older than Sergio.

"Oh you would love the twenty-first century. It's got televisions the size of your wall there, personal phones that fit in your pocket, and this thing called the Internet that...." Sergio broke off as he caught Kat's gaze. "But that's not really relevant at the moment. So maybe back to getting our identities straight?"

Lance was sitting wide eyed, which was partly why Kat had cut Sergio off. No need to tell the man too much. "Televisions as big as a wall, you say? I wonder how they carry something so heavy." His eyes drifted downward, lost in thought, before snapping back to reality.

"Yes, so your identities. I was thinking you could be a distant war contact I once had, and you're from Spain. You're here because a sinister European mafia is on to you because you tried to cut them out of a major drug deal, so you sailed to America to get away and now you're trying to lie low." He stopped and held out his hands, looking from Sergio to Kat. He was completely serious.

"Um..." Kat said. "How about we're just some cousins of yours that moved here looking for a simpler life where we can just relax and enjoy our time with family. We moved from...let's say, Alaska, where it was so cold that I grew worried for the health of our child, so we decided to look for other opportunities in warmer climates. You were gracious enough to let us stay here while we look for work."

"Alaska, huh?" Lance looked thoughtful. "I've never been there, is it nice?"

"We haven't been there either, that's just the story."

"Oh, wow! Oh, you guys are good, you even had me fooled for a second there."

Kat blinked. Lance sure did take some getting used to.

"So we go with that story?" she asked. Sergio nodded but Lance sat back as if considering further.

"Well, I suppose I could find a job in the local factory. They're usually about a hand short. You'll need some kind of cash flow."

"Oh, we have money. That's not a concern," Kat said. She didn't want to mention how they had money yet, but Lance needed to know that they had something at least.

Sergio cut in, "Lance is right though, I'll need to find a job while we're here, otherwise it will look suspicious."

"Quite so," said Lance. "Crumbs, but this story is shaping up to be a good one. Might have even fooled me if I didn't know about it already."

Kat stopped herself from pointing out that it almost had fooled the so-called detective despite being in on the cover story. "So if we have a job, we'll also need a house. I didn't get a good view of the town last night, but it doesn't look big. Is anyone selling?"

"Oh you won't have to worry about that. There's a whole street of new homes that they're trying to sell, just finished building them."

"Huh, convenient," Kat said. "Who's they?"

"There's a woman who runs the real estate here, her name is Norma. I'll take you to see her next week."

"Thank you." Sergio added. "Now about that job, I'm not sure I want to work in a granary. Do you know of anyone hiring mechanical engineers? That's my profession."

"No kidding? Well, I'd hire you myself if I wasn't darn-near broke. Being a detective doesn't pay for much of this." He swept his arm over the room, indicating all the gadgets lying around, the use of which Kat had no clue. "But I could introduce you to Tom. He's got an auto-repair shop and would probably welcome an extra hand. I hear folks sometimes hire him for other mechanical mess ups too. Yeah, Tom might be able to help. He owes me a favor anyway."

"Uh, yeah that sounds okay," Sergio said, shrugging at Kat.

"And what about me?" Kat asked Lance. "I was an English teacher before, maybe I could find work doing something like that?"

"Oh, uh…" Lance looked uncomfortable. "I'm not sure we want to draw suspicion?"

"What suspicion? Your plan was to pretend we were international spies. What is more suspicious than that?"

"Well, begging your pardon ma'am but with you caring for the little one it would be…indecent for you have an occupation while the child needs you."

Kat rolled her eyes. *Of course, they were in the nineteen-forties after all.*

"Well, I can't just stay home all day?"

"Well, of course not, you can do the grocery shopping,

take the kid to the park, do the dish..." but Lance cut off as he glimpsed the look on Kat's face. "Or none of those things. Whatever you want really, that's fine."

"Lance, could you give me and my husband a moment to talk?"

"Sure, no problem!" said Lance, eager for an excuse to escape the uncomfortable tension. "Call me when you need me."

"Are you sure about this?" Kat asked Sergio once they were alone.

"Not entirely, but I definitely feel like we're supposed to stick around for a while."

"But this is California, in the nineteen-forties. We don't know what that's like, or if we can even blend in enough to avoid suspicion. And all this...inherent sexism of the day is probably going to irritate me sooner than later."

Sergio placed a hand on her arm. "I think we can be alright."

"Easy for you to say, you're the one with the pants."

"No, I mean, we won't be here forever, but you saw those...ghosts. That's not normal. I mean, obviously."

Kat nodded. He was right about that. There was something going on here, and with Lance being a member of Argo Force, it was too much of a coincidence that they just happened to arrive at this place and time.

"Okay, I'll go along with it, but if I have to do all the cooking I'm going to scream."

Sergio laughed. "That's okay, dear, I don't want you to cook either."

She punched him in the arm, but found herself laughing anyway.

They called Lance back in, and the man peeked his head

out of his room, as if checking to see the coast was clear. "All decided then?"

"Yes, Lance, you can come back in," Kat said.

"Oh, very good!" Lance exclaimed with almost too much enthusiasm. "This is going to be fun! I've been the only member of Argo Force here for a long time, I almost thought they had forgotten about me."

Lance was an eccentric man, but he definitely appeared to be on their side. Perhaps this wouldn't be so bad after all.

They became too caught up talking to Lance and eating breakfast that they didn't notice the near-invisible apparition watching them from the window.

CHAPTER 2

"THIS WAS THE START OF A LONG AND PAINFUL EXPERIENCE
FOR MY PARENTS. MOTHER WOULD TELL ME ABOUT IT, AND
IT STILL GIVES ME SHIVERS. I JUST DON'T DO GHOSTS.
UNLESS I HAVE TO, OF COURSE."

A month later, and neither Sergio nor Kat had seen any signs of the supernatural since their first night in Greenfield. A lot of other things happened, though. Lance helped Sergio find a job, and they both spoke with Norma, a real-estate agent, about getting a house. She was a sweet lady, almost too sweet, and Sergio couldn't help the feeling that she would stare at him or his wife when they weren't looking.

The house itself was small, and obviously missing a lot of twenty-first century amenities that they were both used to, like air conditioning and a washing machine. But at least they had electrical power, and Kat almost freaked out with joy when she saw the quaint, little rotary-dial phone.

Sergio spent his days working for Tom, a big guy who was happy to outsource most of his work to Sergio so that he could rest and have a beer. It meant that Sergio basically did the work for both of them, but he honestly didn't mind much. Tom was not an overbearing manager, giving Sergio the freedom he needed. He spent most of his time repairing old cars and farm tractors. Or at least, they were old compared to what he was used to. He enjoyed the work. It brought him back to his younger days experimenting with his dad's old vehicle in Argentina.

But seeing as Tom's shop was the only mechanical repair shop in town, people often came with other mechanical problems, everything from a toaster that wasn't working, to problems with the machinery at the granary.

That was where Sergio was headed now. A fellow had called in with a request for a mechanic to take a look at their new tech. The granary recently purchased a large amount of grain-drying equipment and no one there appeared to have any clue how to set it up.

And so they called for Tom, who sent Sergio.

To be honest, he didn't have the faintest clue how some of this machinery worked. He was a mechanical engineer, but his specialty had been in robotics parts. He knew nothing about farming. But given the era they were living in, most of the machinery was so simple that it didn't take him long to find the problem. It was easy work, and that was enough for now.

He arrived at the granary and shook hands with a man called Joel, who had called him in.

"I thought Tom was coming himself?" Joel frowned as Sergio parked the truck.

"He has...other things on his workload. I'm his new employee. Well, new for the last few weeks, that is."

Joel looked him up and down. "We don't get many new people around here. You sure you're up for the job? Lot of this equipment is pretty high-tech."

Sergio grinned. "Believe me, I'm an expert at the high-tech stuff."

"I don't recognize your accent, whereabouts are you from?"

Sergio pursed his lips. He hoped this part wouldn't make a difference. "Argentina originally, but I've spent most of my life here in the States, on the east coast."

Joel considered that. "Hmm. Well, if you can help out with the equipment I guess I don't care where you're from. I'll show you to it."

He brought Sergio to a small clearing where a bunch of shiny new parts lay spread out on the ground.

"We've typically dried our grain by laying it out on the ground, which works well enough," explained Joel. "But this here machine should, in theory, allow us to dry four times as much grain in the same time."

Sergio surveyed the equipment and swallowed. It wasn't that he didn't know how it went together. He was sure he could figure that out. But these pieces were so huge that it was going to make the assembly much more complicated.

"Can I have some of your men help, with the heavy lifting I mean?"

"Of course, you can have all the help you need. Just tell them what to do and they'll do it."

Sergio liked Joel, he seemed a reasonable fellow, and low on his prejudices. Grabbing a few tools from the truck, Sergio began to get to work. He soon identified the major components in the drying equipment and, with the help of a few men, began piecing them together.

It was long work. The sun was high in the sky when Joel finally called for a break. Sergio wiped the sweat off his forehead and gratefully went inside the small barn next to the granary for a drink of water and a moment to lie against a wooden post and shut his eyes.

He was tired, but in a good way. He smiled as a few of the workers patted him on the back. They were making progress and that encouraged everyone working on it.

Taking a sip from his drink, he leaned his head back and took a deep breath. Maybe he and his family could live a normal life here, despite the time jump. This wasn't so bad.

A shadow in the rafters caught his attention. Sergio squinted, wondering if he had just imagined it. But no, there it was again. A small, dark ripple of light. It appeared almost like the way light was distorted on a hot road, except darker. As Sergio looked closer, he could see it had the outline of a person. But there was no one up there.

He blinked, and the shadow disappeared. What had just happened?

The apparition troubled him as he got back to work. It was the first abnormality he had seen since they arrived a month ago. He had just begun to think that maybe life would get back to a semblance of normal. Too optimistic it seemed.

He heard a loud grumble as a tractor started up near him. He kept at his work without looking up. One or two of the farm hands were frequently out on the tractor or another piece of motorized farming equipment. This farm was surprisingly well equipped for such a small town, and one in the nineteen-forties at that.

The noise grew louder, and a voice called out, "Hey, who started the tractor!"

Sergio looked up then. The tractor was moving right for him, fast!

And there was no one driving it.

Before Sergio could react, two hands pushed him hard. He fell just out of harm's way as the tractor rolled by the spot where he had been working.

"Yagh!" the man who had pushed Sergio cried out as the tractor barrelled into him, crushing half the man's body.

Sergio only stood there, horrified. If he had stood there a second longer, it would have been him.

But the needs of the man soon pushed any thoughts of his own survival away. He had to get this man to a hospital.

The thrum of the motor brought Sergio's thoughts in another direction. The tractor was still moving, with no one on it. But instead of moving straight ahead like he expected, it began a slow turn.

Sergio bit his lip. This was not a normal tractor malfunction. There was something guiding that machine, and it wasn't human. He thought back to the shimmering dark mirage he had seen in the barn. Could the two instances be related?

The tractor was coming back around, heading for Sergio again. By this time, the handful of remaining workers were shouting and hurrying to help the injured man. But the tractor was coming right for them.

On a hunch, Sergio moved away from the injured man. As he suspected, the tractor turned so that it was on course to hit him. At least he could draw it away from the others.

Sergio from a year ago would have been freaking out. But after facing killer drones, monsters, and secret murder agents from another dimension, a rogue tractor seemed like nothing at all. Still, he felt his heart pump as it approached.

He readied himself. This was going to be tricky.

The tractor roared as it reached him, but lucky for Sergio, the lumbering machinery couldn't react as fast as he could. He spun out of the way as the tractor arrived. Then before it could turn, he leapt onto the side, barely managing to stay atop the thing as it moved.

The air was cold all of a sudden. He thought he could see his breath in the brief seconds before he lodged himself in the driver's seat. They were in the middle of California.

Never mind being the month of February, it never got cold here.

But Sergio quickly forgot about that. The tractor was beginning to sway from side to side, as if trying to throw Sergio off. But thankfully, Sergio had a good grip, and the tractor wasn't capable of making sharp turns.

He had never been on a tractor before, but Sergio quickly figured out how to turn the engine off. He turned the keys and the tractor sputtered, kept rolling for a few yards, then died.

Sergio breathed a sigh of relief. He was almost certain turning the tractor off would not work, given the odd way it was already behaving. What would he have done if the engine kept running?

The air grew warmer again, which further comforted Sergio. But his comfort was short lived as he ran back to the granary and found the man who had saved him earlier. The others were standing around him, hats off, looking solemn.

"He was too far gone," muttered Joel. "We couldn't save him."

"I...I'm so sorry," muttered Sergio. He couldn't help but think this was his fault. The tractor had pursued him after all. Perhaps if he had been more vigilant.

"Don't be. It's not the first time our equipment has acted up."

"You mean, this has happened before? A tractor spontaneously starting itself?"

"Well, I don't know if it ever got this bad, I honestly can't remember. But we've seen plenty of weird crud around here, that's for sure."

"What was his name?" Sergio asked. He needed to know.

"Ah..." the man paused almost like he didn't know. "Trevor, that was it. Good man. He'll be missed."

He said it so matter-of-factly that Sergio almost called him out on it. But no, seeing death affected people in different ways. It was not Sergio's first time seeing someone die. He wouldn't judge someone for seeming unabashed.

"I think that'll be all for today," Joel continued. "Why don't the rest of you head home, enjoy the comfort of your wives if you have 'em. Nothing like someone dying to give you a fresh perspective on life and living. I'll tend to Trevor."

Sergio frowned. Joel had said all of that in an emotionless, monotone voice. Maybe he really didn't care. "Um...okay, I'll just come back tomorrow then to finish the job."

"I appreciate that," said Joel. He was still looking at Trevor, lying on the ground.

"Okay then." Sergio turned and went back to Tom's truck, which he used to drive back to the shop. From there he walked home, which was only a few blocks away. While he walked, he tried to clear his head. It was still spinning from everything that had just happened. And the weird part was, it almost felt like a dream, like it hadn't really happened. Should he pinch himself? Wasn't that what people did if they thought they were dreaming? But no, who did that anyway?

Before he knew it, he was back at the tiny home that he and Kat had bought. It was a quaint little place, but brand new. And it had a nice "homey" feel to it, a warmth that made it feel good to return home.

He opened the door, and Kat emerged from a back room, holding Alice. "You're back early."

"Yeah..." Sergio mulled over how he was going to tell Kat what happened. Knowing her, she might not take it very well. But in the end, he realized that he couldn't hold back. Word about Trevor's death would spread quickly in a town this small. Better Kat found out from him. "There was an accident at the granary."

And he told her everything, even mentioning the strange apparition he had seen in the barn. Kat listened carefully, not interrupting, but concern slowly wrinkling her face.

"I'm glad you're safe," she said when he finished. "But do you really need to go back tomorrow?"

Sergio nodded. "Whatever this thing was, I don't think it's limited to farming equipment. I mean, you were there when we first arrived, you saw those...things. There's something not right here."

Kat had nothing to say to that. She just kept bouncing Alice up and down in her arms. The girl was looking sleepy. Sergio smiled at his daughter. She was the reason for all of this. Not just for getting them sent back in time, and for all of their troubles with Invergence, but for increasing the love that he had for his family. She made it all worth it.

"Lance came by today," Kat said, changing the subject. "He said he has a few toys he wants you to look at. He can pay for them too."

"I'll check with him tomorrow." Sergio didn't really care about the pay. They still had their Argo Force cash and checkbook that somehow regenerated all the money they needed for whatever time they lived in. But he enjoyed working on some of Lance's projects. Some were a bit outlandish, but others were legitimately fun. The last time he had gone to visit, Lance had set him working on a thermometer that could measure your stress levels. The thermometer had been over three feet long. It was very Doc Brown of Lance, if Doc Brown had also been a detective and master of multiple martial arts.

"You know, I was thinking about Lance," he told Kat. "I know the guy is a bit eccentric, but he's also a good fighter.

You've seen him." Kat nodded, but she was frowning. Best to get this over with. "I was thinking, maybe we could train with him a bit, learn a few defensive moves, you know? It might help if we have another tractor incident."

"How is martial arts going to help you fight a tractor?" Kat looked at him shrewdly.

"I mean, bad example, but I just think it wouldn't hurt."

"I don't know, Sergio. I don't want us to be fighting...whatever this is. I don't want to be looking for trouble."

"We wouldn't look for trouble, obviously," Sergio said. "I'm just saying we should be prepared."

"I'll think about it," Kat said. "But no roaming the streets like a superhero or anything."

"I...what? What gave you that idea?" Sergio laughed. Unfortunately, the idea had occurred to him. He would have to hide his drawings for a potential superhero costume. If certain members of Argo Force got to have a nice suit and cape, why couldn't he?

Kat gave him a look that suggested she knew exactly what he was thinking, but shrugged. "I suppose it wouldn't hurt. But we can talk about this later. I need to put Alice down for the night."

Sergio got to his feet. "Let me do it. You've been with her all day."

Kat relaxed in her chair, her shoulders slumping. "Would you? I appreciate it. She's been upset today. But I just fed her before you arrived so she's sleepy." Kat returned to bouncing Alice up and down in her arms.

Sergio gently took Alice from Kat, trying his best not to disturb her. Sadly, Alice woke and began crying in a tired sort of way, not full wails, but a soft discomfort. Sergio did his best to comfort the girl, but it turned out she needed cleaning. So he changed her diaper and was pleased when

Alice's mood changed. She smiled as she looked at Sergio and put her arms out indicating she wanted to be held.

Sergio picked his daughter up, holding her and rocking her. She was starting to get heavy, now that she was over a year old.

"Once upon a time..." he found himself saying. "There was a young man, named Luke Skywalker. And he wanted more than anything to get away from the boring life he had as a moisture farmer on a desert planet."

He knew Alice was still too young to understand his story. But that didn't stop her from looking at him, listening to the sound of his voice. Besides, this was Star Wars, which technically wouldn't exist for a few more decades. So in the absence of the actual films, Sergio was duty-bound to make sure his daughter was familiar with the saga.

"One day, he met two little droids. Those are like robots that are really smart. Or at least, R2-D2 was really smart, the other one worried a lot."

He continued telling the tale, but only got as far as explaining that Ben Kenobi was really Obi-Wan Kenobi before Alice's eyes were shut. Sergio placed her in the small crib they had purchased a few weeks ago, and stood there observing his daughter for a few moments, watching the way her chest rose and fell as she slept. At risk of waking her up, he leaned over and gently kissed Alice on the forehead.

Ghosts or no ghosts, he was going to protect this girl as best he could. He would do anything to recreate moments like these. Quiet, special moments. They made all the fussing, the diaper cleaning, and all the bad days worth it.

Smiling to himself, he closed the door to Alice's room, and went next door to be with Kat.

CHAPTER 3

K at was beginning to believe that they might just enjoy a normal life in Greenfield. Sure, there was that frightening situation when they first arrived. And then that incident with the tractor at Sergio's work, but in the weeks since then, nothing strange or unusual had happened.

Spring was starting to arrive. While winter had never been that cold here in this small town in California, Kat could appreciate the warm, dry feeling of the sun on her skin. She was out with Alice in her stroller, walking along the streets of Greenfield, heading to a small park near the center of town.

A nice day like today, and the park was full of people. Well, at least as full as it could be considering the town's small population. Several other mothers were there, with the older kids running across the park, and many of the younger ones in strollers like Alice, or in their mother's arms. Despite being a little too gender stereotype-ish for Kat's taste (she didn't see a single man in the park) it was the closest thing she had to living a normal life.

Finding a bench in the grass, she sat down and removed Alice from her stroller. The girl was eager to see and explore the park, as much as she could given her still limited mobility. Kat set her down and let Alice hold the edges of the bench for support. The girl looked all around her, her golden hair driven in the slight breeze.

This. This was nice.

Kat allowed her thoughts to wander, whilst keeping an eye on Alice. After two months of remaining in the same location, they had seen no sign of Invergence. Kat was pretty sure they had lost them for good this time. In the last year, they had never been able to remain in one place for longer than a few weeks without Invergence inevitably finding them. This time, though, they were still here.

Travelling through time certainly seemed to have its advantages, even though the technology was limited here, and the social norms were certainly archaic compared to what she was used to. But overall, it was a nice change from constantly running for her life.

Of course, the apparitions they had seen on their arrival, and Sergio's encounter with a tractor that ran itself, still troubled Kat to no end. As much as she loved living a quieter life, she had the suspicion that it would not remain that way. And though she didn't want to admit it, she knew that Michael, that Founder from Argo Force, had probably sent them here for a reason.

She still held a grudge against Argo Force. Not only had they left Kat and Sergio running for their lives for a year, but they had sent them here with no explanation of why. What was wrong with just explaining these things? It would certainly make their time here a lot easier.

Alice was on her hand and knees in the grass, speeding away as fast as her small appendages would carry her. Kat stood once Alice was a few yards away to bring her back. Alice protested but soon forgot her troubles as a bee buzzed by, distracting her inquisitive mind.

When Kat returned to the bench, she was surprised to find it occupied. A young boy, maybe five or six years old sat in the place Kat had just vacated. He had mousy brown hair and freckles on his face. His mouth was turned in a frown, and he didn't look up at Kat as she approached.

"Oh hello," Kat said. "What's your name?"

The little boy glanced at Kat, but didn't say anything. Kat took a spot on the bench next to the boy, allowing Alice back on the ground. The girl promptly began crawling in another direction like a speeding turtle.

"Where's your mother?" she asked the young boy, glancing around. She couldn't see anyone nearby. "Are you lost?"

The boy looked at her and shook his head. Okay, well at least he could understand Kat.

She bent to stop Alice from putting a bunch of dirt in her mouth. When she sat back down on the bench, this time with Alice in her arms, she looked back at the boy to see him smiling for the first time.

"This is Alice." Kat bounced the girl on her knee. "Say hi, Alice!"

Alice clearly wanted back to the ground, but Kat thought better of it for now. The boy still stared at Alice like he had never seen a baby before.

"Can you tell me where your parents are?" Kat probed again. She didn't think it was good for this boy to be alone.

The boy shook his head.

"Do you know where your parents are?"

No response.

Kat sighed. "Well, maybe I can help you find them." She

stood and began putting Alice back in the stroller. The girl began to cry, upset that her exploration had been cut short.

A small hand grabbed Kat's arm as she was strapping Alice in. The little boy was shaking his head, and holding onto her arm for dear life.

"What is it?" she asked. "You want to find your parents, don't you?"

The boy shook his head. Kat pursed her lips. She hoped the boy was well treated at home. He didn't look like he had any bruises or anything, so she could rule out physical abuse. At least in any serious capacity. Maybe if...

"Simon! Simon!" Kat turned to see a woman with perfectly shaped blonde hair running in their direction. "Oh Simon, there you are, I was worried sick!" As she approached, Kat recognized her. It was Norma, the woman who had sold them the house.

The boy, Simon, almost appeared to shrink against Kat's leg. He clearly did not like Norma.

"Hello Norma, nice to see you here."

"Huh? Oh yes, sorry I didn't recognize you for a moment." She turned back to the boy. "Come on Simon, it's time to go home for some lunch."

The boy didn't move.

"So I take it you're his mother then? I didn't know you had children."

Norma glanced at Kat, her eyebrows furrowed. "Just the one I'm afraid. And while I'm grateful that you kept him here, I really don't appreciate you interacting with him. He's a frail child and needs a delicate touch."

Kat raised one eyebrow. "I don't think there was any harm done." Simon was still clutching one of her legs. Why was he so hesitant to join his mother?

"I'm sure." Norma pursed her lips. "Come now, Simon."

Kat gave Simon an encouraging shove, before he finally, reluctantly left her side. He took small steps to his mother, his head hanging as he walked. Kat didn't like this at all.

Norma grabbed the boy by his shirt and was about to walk away when Kat said, "You know, I never got to thank you for finding us that house. It really is lovely."

"Oh...yes dearie, no trouble at all. I'm glad to see you're settling in. We don't get too many newcomers here."

"Yes, so we've heard."

"And it's nice to see you here, attending to your motherly duties."

That stopped Kat short. "What exactly do you mean by that?"

"Well, I just mean that you're spending your time doing sensible things like tending to your child's needs, rather than...well. Let's just say I've seen you talking to that man Lance from the station. Now I'm sure it's none of my business, but..."

"You're right, it's not," Kat cut in. *Who did this woman think she was?*

"I'm sorry dear, my apologies." Norma grabbed her son's arm and looked like she was preparing to leave. "I'll let you be on your way, I'm sure your husband will be home soon, and you'll need some time to prepare dinner."

That was too much for Kat. "Is that where you're going? To take care of your darling husband." She couldn't keep the sarcasm out of her voice.

"Oh, I don't have a husband, dearie. He died in the war."

Kat nearly cursed herself. She hadn't meant to be insensitive. This was the culture of the day after all, it was something she would have to learn to ignore if she wanted to live a normal life here. Yet she did wish she could wipe that smug smile off of Norma's face. "I'm sorry, I didn't mean to offend."

"No offense taken, dearie." Norma held that over-polite smile. "It just means I'm in the market. I can't keep running the real estate business by myself for much longer. I'm a woman after all, and much more capable of other things. I'm perfectly content to let the men handle the boring jobs."

"I'm sure you are." Kat said dryly. The woman didn't seem at all upset over the death of her husband. She talked about finding a new one like going grocery shopping.

"Well then, I must be going." Norma hitched up her skirts and began walking with her son to the nearest park exit. Simon took one last look at Kat before turning back in the direction they were walking. There was no emotion on his face anymore.

That woman. She had always thought the realtor had a fake cheerfulness to her, but she originally thought that was just part of the act to sell a home. Turned out the woman was sickeningly sweet.

And as much as Kat wanted a normal life here in this small town in the nineteen forties, she'd be hanged if she let all that sexist garbage dictate how she lived her life. Perhaps she would find a job? But even as she thought it, she knew that wouldn't happen here. There weren't enough jobs for the men as it was. There was little chance anyone would hire a woman in this decade. To Kat's knowledge, Norma was ironically the only employed woman in town, and only because she owned her own business. Maybe Kat could start a business?

She pondered the ideas as she pushed the stroller back home with Alice. They didn't live too far from the park, so it only took a few moments to get there. It was only mid after-noon, but she saw many of the other mothers heading home as well. Probably to do as Norma suggested and cook for their husbands. *She wasn't a bad wife for making her husband cook after a long day of work, was she?* Sergio said he enjoyed cooking, that it relaxed him and reminded him of his family in Argentina. Kat was a lousy cook anyway.

Kat pushed aside her internal conflict as she and Alice arrived at the house. Once inside, she fed Alice some mashed carrots, which the girl did not like, and put her down to sleep, which the girl would not do. She wailed and cried the moment Kat disappeared. By the time Kat succeeded in getting Alice to calm down, it was almost time for Sergio to come back home.

Sure enough, she heard the door open and the footsteps of her husband. Leaving Alice alone in her crib, she tiptoed out the door and greeted her husband with a kiss, but putting a finger to her mouth to indicate they should speak softly so as not to wake Alice.

"How was work?" she asked. *That was a normal family-life thing to say, right?*

"It was fine," Sergio said softly. "Someone brought in a car that was so busted we pretty much told the guy he should buy a new car. But he insisted on this one, so we're basically replacing all the parts. Then I went to the granary and...honestly it's all a blur. I just want to sit down for a bit."

Kat smiled. She liked this part. The boring part. Boring meant peaceful.

"How was your day?" Sergio put away his jacket and took off his shoes.

"It was...interesting." Kat told him about Norma, the little boy Simon, and the way he appeared scared of his own mother. She also told him about Norma's rather old-fashioned views on gender roles.

"Huh, well we are in the nineteen forties." Sergio sat on

the couch, and Kat sat next to him. "The war ended just a few years ago. People are having babies left and right, even here in this small town. I suppose we can't expect much better. You know I don't expect any of those things of you, right?"

Kat nodded and smiled, placing her head on his chest. "I know."

"Also, you said that kid's name was Simon? You don't suppose..."

"No," Kat shook her head. "I thought of that, and he'd be about the right age, but there have to be plenty of Simons his age in America. I mean, what would be the odds?"

"I don't know, after last year, I tend to believe less in coincidences than I used to."

Kat would give him that. She didn't like how Argo Force had seemingly abandoned them over the last year, but there were a lot of coincidences that worked in their favor. The first of which was their encounter with Simon, an elderly minister who also happened to be a member of Argo Force, albeit a minor member like Lance. He had been the first to instill hope in the Rios family, hope that they could make it against Invergence, hope of a promising future for Alice. But even those few good weeks had come to an end.

They sat in silence for a while, Sergio's arm around her. Her head rising and falling with his chest.

"I think you should train with Lance," Kat said after several minutes.

"What?" Sergio looked down at her face.

"I do. You're right, it makes sense to be prepared."

"Wow, uh. That's great!" Kat could see the excitement building in Sergio's face.

"I have one condition."

"What's that?"

"I'm going to train with you."

Sergio took a moment to process that, but soon his face lit up even more. "Awesome! We can be like Mr. and Mrs. Smith. Only without the killing each other. Okay, bad example. Maybe more like Superman and Wonder Woman, when they were a power couple!"

Kat smiled. She liked it when he geeked out like this. "Just as long as I don't have to cook."

"Oh, absolutely, let me handle that. In fact, I should get on that right now." He stood and made his way to the kitchen. Calling back, he said, "Did we run out of pickles?"

Okay, so maybe life wouldn't be exactly normal, at least not by current cultural standards. But it was a life Kat could appreciate. Sure, they would start training with a slightly crazy martial artist, and they were undoubtedly still being pursued by an evil alternate reality organization with access to monsters. And of course, there was no denying that Alice was going to grow up to be a very special person. But they loved each other, and they helped each other, and that was normal enough for Kat.

TRUE TO HER WORD, Kat had called Lance and told him that they would like to learn martial arts. Lance agreed emphatically and told them to meet him at an old barn a few blocks away. Sergio had finished work early, so they decided it couldn't hurt to just start that day.

They brought Alice with them, since they had no babysitter to look after the girl. Sergio had suggested they have separate training sessions with Lance, so the other could take care of the baby, but Kat insisted that their first lesson should include both of them. At least for now.

Perhaps with future lessons, they could alternate. They were paying Lance, so he had no problems with the extra lessons.

As they entered the barn, Kat took in her surroundings. It was a large building, with bits of hay scattered across the dirt floor. Though it smelled a bit musty, it looked like this barn hadn't been in use for a while, at least not for livestock. The ground looked soft and clean. Or at least as clean as a dirt floor could be. There was no sign of Lance.

"Perhaps we're a bit early," Sergio suggested. Kat glanced around, pushing Alice along in her stroller.

"I'm sure he'll be along in a moment."

"HEEEYYYAAAAA!" Kat and Sergio spun as a man with a mask jumped out of the shadows at them. Sergio immediately reached for a knife that he kept on his person, but Kat paused to look at the attacker.

She relaxed her shoulders and tilted her head in an expression of annoyance. "Not funny, Lance."

"Your first lesson!" said Lance, with the mask still on. "Always expect the unexpected."

"We got it." Sergio looked a bit more flustered than he would have cared to admit. "We got that one, we have learned our lesson, now take off the mask please. You look like Jason Voorhees."

"Who's Jason Voorhees?" Lance asked as he took the mask off.

"You'll find out in a few decades."

"I see. Well then, are you ready for lesson two!" He spoke with a dramatic flare, like a circus leader. That was going to get old real quick if he kept it up.

"Lance, it's okay, you can drop the dramatics. We just want to learn." Kat folded her arms, letting him know that they weren't here to waste time. Since first meeting Lance two months ago, they had learned that if they gave him an inch he would take a mile. They needed to keep him focused.

"Ah...okay well, that is to say, I'm not exactly sure where to begin. No one has ever asked me to train them before."

"Wait, no one? But we've seen you, you're amazing at it!"

Lance blushed. "Not everyone at the station appears to recognize my talents like you two."

"They haven't seen you fight off ghosts," said Sergio.

"Well I suppose not, but that doesn't change the fact that I'm not sure where to start."

"Why don't you start the way you learned martial arts?" Kat offered.

"Oh, no you wouldn't like that, not at all. Though I suppose..." Lance broke off, running his hand over his chin. "Yes, we could begin with that. It's not a bad place to start."

"What is?" Sergio asked apprehensively.

"Well, it's going to be tough. Not at all easy for a beginner."

"Can you just tell us please?" Kat tried her best to stay patient, but sometimes it was difficult with Lance.

"Footwork."

"What?"

"Yes, footwork. A great place to start."

"Oh," Sergio looked relieved. "Well, that doesn't seem so bad."

"Oh, you just wait. You see, the key to proper training in any physical discipline is muscle memory. There's even something magic about it, I hear. It's been a technique passed on from the ancient masters of speed and grace."

"So what would you like us to do?" Kat asked.

"Well, let's start with a few stances. These will help you keep your balance."

Lance began to show them a few steps. Kat and Sergio

imitated what he showed them. Despite Lance's statement that he didn't know where to start training them, he soon got into the spirit of things. He moved to correct their stances, showing them how to keep a solid footing on the ground.

It was clear he knew what he was talking about, even if he was a strange teacher. Kat did her best to follow along, and didn't even get mad when Lance tried to push them both over, to prove that their footwork wasn't right yet.

Mostly though, he just had them move from one stance to another, twirling around the barn as they did so. It didn't take long before Kat was beginning to feel fatigue build up in her legs. So she was surprised, an hour later when Lance called out. "Okay, looks like we're good on the warmup. Time to get into the meat of it."

"Wait, what?" Kat and Sergio said together.

"Oh sure, you see muscle memory is just the beginning. We need to build up your strength. I've got a series of exercises that I do each morning, that we're going to do now."

And so they began with a series of pushups, core workouts, running in place, and a lot of other things that made Sergio and Kat wish they had rethought this whole training thing. And Lance expected them to do this every day?

Both parents were more than glad to pause to tend to Alice, who was upset that she had been left alone in the stroller. They let her out for a while, to explore the barn, but that meant taking more breaks to keep her out of trouble. While Kat and Sergio were perfectly okay with this, Lance was less so. For all his distraction in getting started, he was hyper focused now. He not only spotted Kat and Sergio as he ran them through his series of exercises, but he did the work himself too, making it look easy.

The sun was almost down when they heard a loud

beeping noise. It was Lance's watch, or at least something that looked vaguely like a watch. It was one of Lance's inventions, the purpose of which, Kat and Sergio had no idea.

"Oh, sorry, it's getting late. I have to go."

"Where are you headed?" Kat asked. To her knowledge, Lance didn't do much outside of his own home. He didn't have a significant other, and didn't hang out at bars or anything. Not that there was more than one bar in town anyway.

"Oh, I just need to go take care of those ghosts again. Like the ones you saw when you first arrived."

"What? You mean there's more of them?" Sergio asked. His face had paled, and he was unconsciously rubbing his face, undoubtedly remembering the time that a ghost had touched him, nearly giving him frostbite.

"Oh yes, they come back every month."

"Every month!" Now even Kat was taken aback. Why hadn't Lance said anything?

"Yes, but I told you this, didn't I?" Kat and Sergio both shook their heads. "But I was sure I did. No matter, it's no problem at all. I've been taking care of them for about three years now. Ever since the war ended."

"This has been going on for three years?"

"Yep, though I admit I still don't know what's causing it. They keep coming back at the same time every month."

"Are they the same...erm...ghosts, or are they different each time?" Sergio kept rubbing his arm.

"Hard to tell sometimes, but I believe they're the same. I've been at this long enough to recognize a few faces."

Kat shivered. She didn't need the reminder that this was not a normal life they were living. Something was happening in this town and she couldn't quite make out what it was. But all of it made her uncomfortable, from the sickeningly sweet way in which Norma berated her, to the silent boy, to the ghosts themselves. To paraphrase Shakespeare, something was rotten in Greenfield.

"Anyway, I have to be going. It'll take me a small while to get to the foothills," Lance said again. He grabbed some of his things and made for the barn door.

"Hey Lance," Kat called after him. "What exactly happens if you don't fight them?"

Lance's face sobered. "Then they enter the town. And believe me, you don't want to see that happen."

Kat swallowed as Lance retreated. She picked up Alice and gently placed her back in the stroller. Alice went along willingly, appearing a bit tired from running around the barn all evening.

You and me both, child. Kat thought as she felt her own muscles protest while they walked home.

No, life for them would probably never be normal again. Kat was beginning to accept that, though she still did not like it. However, that didn't mean they had to lay down and take it. They could face their problems head on, and perhaps Lance could help with that, for all his eccentricities. Sooner or later, they would find out what was causing these so-called ghosts to appear in Greenfield. And maybe they could stop it.

CHAPTER 4

"MOM ALWAYS WANTED A NORMAL LIFE. UNFORTUNATELY
THAT..,OH WAIT, I SAID THIS ALREADY. MY BAD."

Sergio rose for the morning and stretched. Kat lay still asleep as she usually did, so Sergio did his best not to disturb her as he made his way to the bathroom.

He ran through the same morning routine he had kept for years. Or was it months? Anyway, soon he was showered, his teeth were brushed, he gobbled some leftovers for breakfast, went in to kiss Kat and Alice goodbye, and he was out the door.

It was a good day, the sun was shining, the air was crisp. It was already pretty warm here in sunny California. Remarkable since they had only been here a month.

Sergio stopped short. It had been more than a month, right? No, they had just arrived. Maybe two months? He tried to remember the date. Today is...April...no, February?

One of the neighbors drove by and waved. He waved back and continued on his way to Tom's shop. What had he been worried about a moment before?

He didn't remember so he continued on, whistling as he did so. After walking just a few blocks from his house, he arrived at Tom's garage.

"Hey, I have a special assignment for you," Tom said once Sergio arrived. "Them folks at the granary have some new grain-drying machines they want set up. None of it makes sense to me, but you seem to know your way around the more advanced stuff. Would you head over to take a look? They pay well."

"Sure thing, boss." *Sure thing, boss? Since when did he talk like that.*

He packed up the tools he thought he'd need in the truck, then headed out towards the granary. He'd never been there before, but he knew some of the guys who...

Something was feeling very familiar about all this. Sergio frowned. As he pulled into the granary, he could have sworn that he had been here before. He'd seen the granary from a distance of course, but to his knowledge he had never actually set foot inside.

A big man approached him. Joel, the landowner. "I thought Tom was coming himself?" Joel frowned as Sergio parked the truck.

"He has...other things on his workload. But I know my way around equipment so he sent me."

Joel looked him up and down. "You sure you're up for the job? Lot of this equipment is pretty high tech."

Sergio grinned. "Believe me, I'm an expert at the high-tech..." He trailed off. Something didn't feel right here. Hadn't he been here and said these things before?

"You okay, son?"

Sergio pursed his lips. "Uh...yeah, yeah everything is fine."

Joel considered that. "Hmmm. Okay, well if you can help out I guess it doesn't matter who is here to help."

He brought Sergio to a small clearing where a bunch of shiny new parts lay spread out on the ground.

"We've typically dried our grain by laying it out on the ground, which works well enough," explained Joel. "But this here machine should, in theory, allow us to dry four times as much grain in the same time. I...are you alright?"

Sergio had a hand to his head, and his breathing was increasing. He had definitely been here before. But why on Earth couldn't he remember how or when? He distinctly remembered seeing these pieces here before. But from the sound of things, this was the first time they were installing these materials.

"Um...ah, yeah. Can...can I have some of your men help, with the heavy lifting I mean?"

"Of course, you can have all the help you need. Just tell them what to do and they'll do it."

Joel barked an order and several other employees came walking over. "If you need anything, just tell these guys, Trevor here can come get me if there are any problems."

"Hi Trevor, good to..."

"Tarnations son, just what is going on. You've been acting strange all morning."

This time Sergio was staring at Trevor, one hand frozen in the act of reaching forward to shake the man's hand. This...this man shouldn't be here. He didn't know why, but something about this worker, Trevor, was completely wrong.

"I...I'm sorry sir, I ah, I didn't sleep well last night. I'll get to work right away."

Trevor put his hand down, awkwardly. Unshaken.

For now, Sergio was just going to ignore what he had seen. Something wasn't right, but he had a job to do, and he was going to do it.

He spent the next few hours cataloging and arranging the pieces for the granary's new grain-drying apparatus. He did his best to ignore the feeling that he had done this before, and just kept to his work. Still, he somehow, miraculously made good time assembling the pieces. He seemed to know exactly what to do without studying the pieces. This unsettled him, but he must have just been thinking quick on his feet that day. Yeah, that must have been it. His familiarity with modern technology must be giving him an edge working with this stuff.

Lunch arrived and Joel was generous to give them all something to eat, along with some cool lemonade that Sergio accepted gratefully. Taking a moment, he retreated into the barn to cool off.

He thought he saw something in the rafters, but dismissed it. There was nothing there. Why would there be?

Lunch ended and he made his way back to his work. He...why did he get the feeling that something bad was about to happen? He looked one way, then another. Joel was talking to a few of his men, though Trevor was cleaning down a tractor that one of the others had just brought back in.

In a rush of memories, Sergio remembered! He *had* been here before, doing the exact same things he was doing now. He remembered the tractor and Trevor...Trevor had died. But he was here, now, standing in front of Sergio without a scratch on him. What was going on?

With a rumble, the tractor started up by itself. Trevor backed away as it did so. "What the..." he broke off as the tractor lurched forward. It knocked Trevor down and Sergio heard a sickening crunch as it ran over the man for the second time in Sergio's memory.

People were shouting and running in every direction. All except Sergio. Because he had a good idea of what was coming next.

The tractor made a slow turn and faced him. It felt

almost like a standoff. Sergio didn't know what was possessing the tractor to make it move like it did, but whatever it was, it wanted Sergio dead.

It charged, moving at a speed that Sergio would not have thought possible of a low-tech tractor. But it sped towards him. He held his ground, knowing that running wouldn't make things any better. He had faced this thing before, right? The memory was still cloudy, but yes. If he could just dodge out of the way at the last second and climb on top of the tractor, perhaps he could...

A strong pair of hands grabbed him. He tried to move, and the hands held him fast. Turning he found one of the workers was holding him in the approaching path of the tractor.

"What? Let go of me!"

But the man didn't answer. He only stared straight at the approaching tractor, his eyes almost glazing over.

Lance's training was the only thing that saved Sergio. Instinctively, he removed himself from the man's hold and threw him to the ground using a self-defense technique Lance had taught him earlier. Then he leapt out of the way just as the tractor reached their position. He didn't look to see what happened to the man that held him.

Sergio looked up from his place on the ground. The tractor was turning, albeit slowly. He could stop it if he hurried. Running, he closed the distance between him and the tractor with ease. Since it was turning, he had a good opening to leap onto the tractor from the side, and turn it off. Blessedly, it powered down and came to a slow halt.

Sergio let out a long breath. What had that been about?

He brought the tractor back himself, taking care that he stayed clear of any people.

What he found when he returned to the granary was

Trevor, lying in the dirt, quite obviously dead, like before. Some shouting from where the other worker had held Sergio told him that Trevor wasn't the only one mortally hurt.

The other man's name was Herman. Sergio had worked with him all that day, and he'd seemed pretty nice to him then. What had changed to make him commit suicide by trying to kill Sergio? None of it made any sense.

"I think that'll be all for today," Joel said after they assessed the damage. "Why don't the rest of you head home, enjoy the comfort of your wives if you have 'em. Nothing like someone dying to give you a fresh perspective on life and living. I'll tend to Trevor and Herman."

There it was again, the same monotone voice that Sergio had heard the last time this happened. He was sure, now, that he had been in this same situation before. But how, he could not imagine. Perhaps he should ask Lance about this. That man, as crazy as he might look, seemed to have this town figured out. They just needed to talk to him more about it.

He took the truck back to Tom's garage and walked the rest of the way home. Everything felt...weird. Like he was part of a dream and couldn't wake up. Perhaps that was it. Was he in some crazy nightmare that kept repeating itself? His world certainly felt real.

"Hey love!" Kat said as he walked through the door. "You're back early."

"Yes. And it's the strangest thing."

He then proceeded to tell her everything that had happened, including how it felt like everything had happened before. Like he was living in a repeating dream.

"You know, that's funny because I felt the same way today when I took Alice to the park," she responded when he had finished. "I met a boy there called Simon. He didn't talk, but I was sure I had seen him before."

"How did you know his name if he didn't talk?"

"Oh, his mother arrived and told me. You remember Norma, who sold us the house? Yeah, apparently she has a son we didn't know about. She didn't seem very nice. Said some rather offensive things about my parenting methods, and even implied that I wanted to steal the boy from her. I mean, can you believe that?"

"Add it to the list of weird things happening in this town. Also, you said that kid's name was Simon? You don't suppose..."

"No," Kat shook her head. "I thought of that, and he'd be about the right age, but there have to be plenty of Simons his age in America. I mean, what would be the..."

She trailed off. Sergio recognized it too. They had had this conversation before!

"Oh my." Kat put a hand to her face. "You're right. We have lived this before. I can remember it all now."

"Thank you! I thought it was just me."

"What is happening, Sergio? We've only been here a month, how can we have experienced these things already."

"I don't think we have been here for just a month. It's April right? Didn't we get here in the middle of winter?"

Kat's eyes widened. "You're right now that I think of it."

"I think there's something going on here that might be making us...I don't know, relive part of our lives or something."

"Do you think there are any connections to those apparitions that we fought when we first got here?"

Sergio had almost forgotten about those. "Maybe, I'm meeting Lance tonight. Maybe I can ask him what's going on."

"Okay, but be careful. We don't know if he's somehow wrapped up in all this as well. And after what happened to you when that man tried to keep you in the path of that tractor, we can't trust anyone."

"I agree, though I think Lance is different. I'm not sure how."

"Even so..."

"I'll be careful, love. Don't worry."

He rose and found himself in the kitchen cooking a light stir fry for dinner. He didn't have a lot of time, so he worked as quickly as he could.

Kat brought Alice in, who was just waking up from a nap and rubbing her eyes. Wow, she was getting big, way bigger than Sergio expected for someone who just turned one. He...

Sergio put a hand to his head. Why couldn't he fully realize that they had been in Greenfield for several months now? The moment he thought he'd figured it out, he would go back to thinking that they had just arrived. Though sometimes it also felt like they had always lived in Greenfield. It was a very disconcerting dichotomy of feelings. But Alice's growth didn't lie. She had to be several months over one year now. Sergio thought back to the dates. Yes, they had arrived in January. It was now April. That made Alice about sixteen months old.

Even as Sergio formed the dates in his head, he could feel something pushing back, making him second-guess those dates. The more he thought about their time there, the more his brain seemed to drift into a fog, as if he had a few drinks too many, or stayed up too late.

He finished the stir-fry and distributed what he had onto two plates. Handing one to his wife, he saw Alice reach for it, curious to know what the smell was. Kat grabbed the plate and sat down at their small dinner table, keeping the food just out of reach of their baby girl.

Alice, upset that something was denied her, began to pout and whine. But she looked cute even when pouting. Sergio smiled and searched the cupboard for some baby food. He also grabbed a banana and mashed it up for Kat, who took it and began feeding pieces to Alice, who promptly forgot about her troubles of being denied the stir-fry.

Sergio paused to take it all in. He loved moments like this, moments when he and Kat just clicked and cared for their child without even needing to communicate verbally. Alice had unified them in a way that several years of marriage had not. They were a team now.

Finishing his stir-fry, he wiped his chin with a napkin and stood, taking his plate to wash in the sink. "Well, I need to be going. Love you."

He kissed his wife on his way out. "Be careful," she repeated. He nodded, shook Alice's little hand as a goodbye gesture, grabbed his jacket, and was out the door.

It wasn't until he was halfway to the abandoned barn that his thoughts turned again to the strange repetitions of the day, and how he had trouble remembering how long they had been in Greenfield. Even now he found it difficult to even think about it, which troubled Sergio almost more than the attempt on his life earlier. Something was definitely wrong in Greenfield. He just wished they could figure it out before it caused them any serious harm.

Moments later, and he was at the barn. Lance was there, thankfully not trying to scare him this time. Sergio thought on that for a moment. Just how long had he been training with Lance now? It was hard to tell.

"Ahoy there, Sergio!" Lance greeted him as he approached. "Ready to get started?"

Sergio nodded. "We've been doing your morning exercise routine every day, just like you said."

"Ah good, we'll be increasing that this week."

Sergio felt his shoulders slump. Increase? They had trouble keeping up with what they had. It seemed that Sergio always found himself sore in the mornings. But he said nothing and began running through the footwork techniques that Lance had been training them on. He was pleasantly surprised to see that he was doing rather well. His feet moved almost automatically as Lance dictated, without Sergio having to think about it too hard.

"Great, I see you finally got the hang of Sun Stance and Deer on the Rocks." Lance was nodding his head in approval.

'Finally?' Hadn't Sergio only just started learning those two stances? But the moment he had that thought, Sergio recognized it as the same confusion that had been plaguing him all day. No, when he thought hard about it, he *had* been working on these stances for a while, over a month.

"Lance, I have a question for you." Sergio quit his stances and stood normally. "Have you ever felt like, I don't know, like history is repeating itself? I don't mean the distant past, but more like what's happened recently is happening again?"

Lance looked at him sharply. "You've noticed that, have you?"

"Yes!" Sergio began to feel relief that Lance recognized what he was talking about. "Today, I saw a man die, a man I'm sure actually died a few months ago, or maybe last month. I really don't know. It's like a crazy case of deja vu."

Lance regarded him and nodded. "I was wondering if it

would take you too, or if you would notice. The fact that you did notice something speaks volumes about your strength of will. Your wife notice the same thing?"

"Yes, but what is going on?"

Lance sighed. "To be honest, I still haven't figured it out, see. I've been here for nearly three years and nothing has changed about this town. Nothing, that is, until your family arrived."

"Do you think it has something to do with those...apparitions we saw when we arrived? You said they come every month, right?"

"That they do, and I'm sure they have something to do with it. Too much of a coincidence. But I still know very little. No one here has realized what you have, that nothing changes here."

"But you've realized it too, right? Just like us?"

"Affirmative, but it took a long time before I came to the same conclusions. You've managed to figure it out far faster than I did. I can still feel it, something trying to keep my mind from thinking about time and the problems in this town."

Sergio nodded eagerly, this was exactly what he had been feeling lately. "Do you have any theories?"

Lance shrugged, "A few, but none of them concrete. The only lead I have are them ghosts."

"What about them?"

"Well, when I go to fight them, it...helps to clear my mind. I don't know what it is, but I somehow manage to keep my sanity when fighting them. Matter of fact, tonight is the night. I'll need to head over there soon."

Sergio let his eyes drop to the ground in thought. He still had no idea what any of this meant, but he was starting to form a picture in his head. At the very least, he knew he needed to find out more about these ghosts.

"Can I come with you?"

"What's that?"

"To fight the...ghosts, as you call them. I'd like to help."

Lance rubbed his chin. "Well, I suppose it would never hurt to have someone else along for the ride. What would your wife think of you coming with me?"

Sergio grimaced. She probably wouldn't like it, not one bit. Despite all that had happened since they arrived in Greenfield, Kat was still determined to stay away from trouble if possible. She had only approved of training with Lance to learn self-defense for a last-resort type of situation. But despite all that, Sergio found himself saying, "I'm sure she'll be fine with it. I can help tonight!"

"Well, then I suppose your training for today will include a bit of ghost hunting!" Lance seemed in a much better mood all of a sudden.

"So...uh...where do we start?"

"Well, just follow me."

Lance exited the barn almost at a jog and Sergio had to move quickly to follow. He kept pace until they arrived at Lance's house. Inside, the floor and other surfaces were covered with gadgets and grease, just as it had been when Sergio first arrived in Greenfield.

Lance approached one contraption lying on his table. It was the flamethrower exosuit that Lance had worn that first day when they had seen the ghosts in the foothills.

"This, here, is what I use to get rid of the ghosts. At least temporarily. I still haven't worked out a way to extinguish them for good. I've made it almost entirely of pure iron."

"Wouldn't a lighter metal be better?" Sergio asked. "Even

steel would be strong enough that you wouldn't need as much metal to do the job."

"Son, what do you know about ghosts and iron?"

Sergio thought on that. Aside from the fact that he hadn't considered ghosts to be real, Lance's words tickled something in his memory. A television show he used to watch.

"Isn't iron supposed to repel ghosts? I mean, in the stories at least?"

"That's correct, the stories are true on that point, do you want to know why?"

Sergio nodded, this was getting interesting.

"Well, I still don't know everything about these ghosts, but I've discovered one thing. They crave energy. Or they are energy. Either way, iron acts as a conductor. It absorbs them and sends their essence into the ground using these." Lance pointed to the legs of the exosuit which had two spikes below the feet. "These penetrate the ground and direct the ghost's energy down into the Earth. It's the only thing I've found that works, at least temporarily, to get rid of the ghosts."

"That's why you used fire, not to kill the ghosts, but to attract them with the energy."

Lance nodded, "When the ghosts touched you, and your wife, you felt what?"

"Deadly cold, and numbness."

"They were sucking the energy out of you. If they had continued, you would have died, rapidly."

"Wow, what would happen if they were set loose on the city?"

"You don't want to find out. And this is just a temporary solution, as they reappear every month, but it seems to do the trick for now."

"So why do they crave energy? What purpose does that serve?"

"I don't know, but I have some theories. But that's another story, and we have little time right now. I have a backup suit that you can use if you want."

"Do I?" Sergio exclaimed. "This is the coolest thing anyone has ever asked me to do!"

"So...that's a yes on the spare suit?"

"Affirmative!" Sergio gave him a casual salute for fun, though Lance returned it in all seriousness. Sergio almost laughed, but his own excitement overran his mind. This was it, he was finally getting a chance to be a superhero, even if the circumstances were a bit different than he imagined, more Doctor Strange than Captain America. But regardless, he was going to enjoy this.

He took the spare suit and, after practicing for a few minutes, he and Lance walked toward the foothills. On the way, Sergio was careful to steer them down a different road, one that would keep them from walking in front of his house. He wasn't quite ready to tell Kat about this yet, and he didn't want her finding out the wrong way. Thankfully, Lance didn't ask questions.

Once on the foothills, Sergio could see no evidence of the ghosts.

"We still have a few minutes." Lance looked at his watch.

"Do they always come at the same time?" Sergio was excited but his eyes were wide with anxiety, staring around the clearing for any sign of the apparitions.

"Yes, always. Twenty-one hundred hours."

Sergio looked at his watch and counted down the minutes. At nine o'clock exactly, he heard the first shriek. Heart pounding, he fingered the trigger that would activate the flame thrower.

"Be ready," Lance said, his usually jovial self now more serious than Sergio had seen in a while.

Sergio readied himself, unconsciously adopting Sun Stance as he waited. Faint, ghostly images appeared before him, like afterimages left in your vision after staring at a light. They were here.

Lance activated the flames from his suit, and Sergio quickly did likewise. The ghosts turned in their direction, the firelight reflecting in the dark pools of their haunting eyes.

Then they came. Attracted by the fire's energy, they flew at the duo. Sergio raised his fiery hands high. Flame shot from his hands and scorched the nearest ghost. It screamed, but it was only weakened. Lance had explained that the fire, though attractive to the ghosts, was also too much energy for them to handle all at once. It hurt them as much as it hurt regular people, weakening them and making it easier for the next part.

The ghost was nearly on Sergio now, and he thought he might have a heart attack. His blood pressure was ringing in his ears, and adrenaline coursed through his veins. But remembering Lance's training, he shoved both hands into the ghost, creating contact between the iron spikes attached to his hands and the wispy tendrils of the apparition. It screamed and Sergio saw it disappear an instant later, sucked into the iron and down into the earth.

He avoided the temptation to look down, half expecting the ghost to rise from the ground and drag him down with it. But another ghost was approaching and he turned his attention to face it. A moment later it too was gone.

This wasn't so bad. This was actually kind of fun.

Lance was likewise taking out one ghost after another, far faster than Sergio, who was letting the ghosts come to him. But still, they were mopping up this group of ghosts much more efficiently than the night that Sergio and Kat had originally arrived in town.

Sergio could get used to this. Kat wouldn't like it, and he was going to have to invent some excuse for why he would arrive home late tonight. But he could figure that out later.

Right now, he had some ghosts to shove off.

CHAPTER 5

"AH THE COMFORT OF GOOD FRIENDS..."

K at awoke one morning as she always did. Sergio was already up and nearly out the door. She tended to sleep longer when she could, since she usually had to check up on Alice once or twice in the night. She did this so Sergio didn't have to worry about it. He had work the next day and needed his sleep.

It still kind of bothered her that she couldn't find her own job, and that she was expected to be the traditional mother. That said, Alice needed someone, and there weren't many arms to hold her as consistently as needed. Thankfully, Alice was beginning to become more independent by one-year-old standards. She was happily content in a little playpen as long as she had plenty of toys to occupy her. Large toys of course. Alice had a nasty habit of putting everything in her mouth. Not that this was unusual for children her age, but Alice did seem to do it all too often. Sometimes her curiosity was too much for her own good.

Kat brushed her teeth, prepared a small breakfast using leftovers from the night before, and fed and changed Alice. The little girl cooed as Kat finished securing her clean diaper. Well, at least the girl was generally a happy child. That was more than could be said for some.

Kat continued her morning routine, making sure Alice was content in her playpen before taking a quick shower. Another thing was beginning to bother Kat. She had wanted a normal life, but now everything was beginning to feel...too normal. Her morning routine was just one example. It stood in stark contrast to last year when they had been on the run from Invergence. Back then, a morning routine simply didn't exist. Now, she seemed to move almost on instinct from one task to the next, barely even noticing what she was doing.

She came out of her thoughts to realize that she had left the shower, dressed, and was now preparing Alice for a trip to the park without even realizing it. See, this was the problem. When had Kat even decided to go to the park?

But she supposed it didn't really matter. Alice loved going out and Kat could use the fresh air. It wasn't like going to the park was a bad thing. Right? It was just...it almost felt like Kat was losing control of herself.

She remembered her conversations with Sergio a few weeks ago, when the tractor had mysteriously tried to run him over, for the second or third time since they arrived. Since then, they had kept careful track of the dates and that seemed to help. They no longer felt like they had just arrived in Greenfield. They were much more aware of the problems here, but that didn't stop Kat from feeling like something was still guiding her mind, causing her to think about some things and not think about others.

"Come on, let's go," she said to Alice as she lifted her into a stroller and opened the door. Alice, eager for the trip outside, covered her eyes as they exited the house and the sunlight waved in their faces.

Already seventeen months old, Alice was growing in

intelligence. She could say a few words and both Kat and Sergio were growing fond of talking to her. Sergio especially chatted with Alice into the night, telling her bedtime stories and never dumbing-down his speech to a child's level. Kat liked that about him. He treated Alice like the intelligent girl she was.

"Daw," Alice chirped as she saw a neighbor walking their dog, passing a little girl bouncing a ball on her porch.

"Yep, that's a dog," Kat answered as she pushed the stroller down the street in the direction of the park. Again, she was struck by how familiar everything seemed, and it wasn't just because she had taken Alice to the park several times before now. She could have sworn she had seen that little girl bouncing her ball before, in the exact same driveway.

Everything about this place made her uneasy. Was it just the time period? She couldn't tell. But she wasn't going to let it hurt Alice or anyone in her family for that matter.

When she arrived at the park, she paused. Mothers and children were strewn through the greenery, going about their own business. Kat knew they lived in a small town, but she could have sworn that she'd seen each of these mothers in the same places doing the same things the last time that she had been here, in this park.

Once again, Kat could feel that fog surround her mind, making it difficult to think, difficult to remember why the things she saw were strange. She shook it from her head and found a place to park the stroller and let Alice out for a while.

The little girl was delighted to roam around the park, even if her mother had to pull things from her mouth on occasion. Kat sat on a nearby bench watching her daughter move about, far more nimbly than before. She could remember being here several times now, that much she had managed to remember, despite the fog on her brain. Sergio too was having an easier time remembering their stay, but some things still didn't add up. Like why was Kat even here today? She felt like one moment she had been in the house, and the next in the park, as if no decision had been made.

She arose to get Alice, who had strayed a little too far away. Alice was walking now, to the delight and fear of her parents. A walking Alice meant that she was much more mobile and could find herself wandering when her parents weren't looking. So Kat watched her like a hawk.

When she returned to the bench, she found a young boy standing there, maybe five or six years old. He had mousy brown hair and he was sitting right where Kat had been a few seconds before. She hadn't seen him approach.

"Hi there," she said. "What's your name?"

The question left her mouth, though she was sure she knew this boy. She shook her head as the fog pushed in closer. She had seen this boy before, right?

"I'm Simon." The boy was looking almost hurt, like she should have known that his name was Simon. And indeed, the moment he said it, Kat thought she remembered.

"Oh, that's right. I think I've seen you before. Where is your mother?"

The boy said nothing now, his eyes growing dark. Lifting his feet onto the bench, he clutched his knees to his chest.

"Isn't Norma your mother, is that right?"

The boy nodded.

Kat paused to bring Alice back from another excursion in the wrong direction, then sat down next to Simon, holding Alice this time. Alice started to protest that she couldn't explore anymore, but stopped when she noticed

Simon sitting nearby. She fixated on the boy, slack jawed as she often was when she saw something interesting.

Simon smiled for the first time, and reached a hand to Alice, who did the same and their fingers met. Alice laughed in delight. Kat smiled. It was such a beautiful thing when Alice laughed.

"So where is Norma?" She glanced around, trying and failing to find the real estate agent.

The smile vanished on Simon's face. "I ran."

Kat's eyebrows furrowed. "You ran? Ran from where?"

"Ran away."

"Are you saying you ran away from your mother?" Kat tried to find the woman again, but still didn't see her anywhere. "Why would you run away?"

"Momma hurts."

Kat swallowed. This may be a more serious situation than she realized. "Come here, Simon. I just want to check a few things."

Simon left the bench and came in front of her. Holding Alice in one arm, she used the other to check for any bruises on the boy. She found none, not even the small bruises she might expect on an active young boy playing in the park. Well, so much for that theory.

"How does your momma hurt you, Simon. Could you tell me? I'd like to help so that she doesn't hurt you again."

Simon placed one arm on hers, and Kat gasped, but not because of his touch. Suddenly, the fog that had been there, hovering over her mind, was gone! It was like walking into a warm room and realizing that you had been cold all along. She could think! And it felt good.

She stared at Simon. "Wha...what did you—"

"And just what do you think you're doing!" A voice boomed across the park, making heads turn.

Kat stood up, Alice still in her arms. It was Norma, and she was walking in their direction with fury on her face. Kat felt something tug at her pant leg and looked down to see Simon. He was terrified, trying to hide from his mother behind Kat's leg.

"Simon came to me and I asked him where you were, no harm done."

"Oh I think we all know that's not true. This isn't the first time I've caught you with my boy. What do you want with him?"

"I promise you, he came to me. I only tried to keep him safe until someone came for him."

"A likely story. Come here, Simon."

Simon didn't move. He remained clutched to Kat's side. Kat stated the obvious. "I don't think he wants to go with you."

Norma's face grew redder. "I knew it, I knew you wanted to take him away from me!"

"Take him...now wait one second. Don't turn this around on me. The boy is clearly scared of his own mother. What are you doing to him to make it so?"

"Children lack discipline, they require a firm hand. Without it, they grow up into delinquents. No child enjoys discipline. It's why we call it tough love. But I need not explain these things to you, since you clearly lack the spine to do what is necessary."

Kat felt her face flush. Who did this woman think she was? Putting Alice down in her stroller, she straightened and met Norma's eyes, stare for stare. She didn't even notice the other eyes staring at them from all directions in the park. This woman wanted to make a scene, then they would make a scene.

"He's scared of you. That's enough for me to call a social worker to investigate. I will do it."

Norma laughed. "You'll never find a social worker here, dearie. You might not have noticed, but it's a small town here."

"Then I'll go to the city."

"Mhmm, good luck with that."

"I'm serious! If you're hurting this kid, I swear I'll—"

"You'll do what, dearie? There's nothing you can do. I, on the other hand, am an old friend of the police commissioner in this town. If you don't hand over the boy right now, I'll have you arrested for kidnapping."

Kat glanced around for the first time since the argument started. People were staring at them, even the children. No, they weren't staring at them, they were staring at her, specifically. Kids had stopped playing, mothers had stopped pushing their strollers, everyone was looking at Kat as if to see what she would do.

Kat grimaced. This town...

She turned to face Norma again. "You're not the only one with contacts among the police. And if they hear that you're abusing this boy, you'll never see him again. My friend, Lance—"

And that was when she saw it. For a moment, Norma's eyes flared, literally flared a bright red. Kat stopped midsentence. Had she imagined it? Could it have been a trick of the light? But no, she had definitely seen the woman's eyes turn red, almost like a flame.

Norma took a deep breath, her eyes back to normal. "I think perhaps we've taken this a bit too far, dearie." Her voice was calmer now, composed. "If you really wish it, we can meet at the station tomorrow and discuss it with the kind officers. I'm sure we can sort this out in no time."

Kat was about to give the woman another piece of her mind, when she felt something tug on her pant leg. She looked down to see Simon. He was looking at her, concern on his face.

"I'll go," he said. "I'm not scared."

Kat bent down so she was at his level. "Are you sure, Simon? I don't want you to get hurt again."

"I'm not scared," he said again. That wasn't exactly encouraging to Kat, but before she could say another word, Simon had left her and joined his mother.

"There, that wasn't so bad, was it?" Norma said to Simon. Her voice was back to that sickening sing-song tone. "Now, say goodbye to the nice lady."

Simon raised one hand to wave at Kat. He waved a hand at Alice too.

"I warn you," Kat said as the two were turning away. Norma turned her head back to face Kat. "If I find any evidence that you've been abusing him in any way, I will find a way to ensure that you never hurt him again."

This time, she was sure she saw it. Norma's eyes flashed a brief red. That definitely wasn't just the light. But before Kat could say something, Norma spoke again. "You do what you think is right, girl. I will do the same." And without another word, she turned and led Simon away from the park.

Kat watched her go, then looked at the other spectators in the park. Immediately they turned away and resumed what they had been doing, almost as if they had never stopped. The sound of laughter filled the park as children continued their play. Alice was the only one not making any sound, unusual for her. She was staring off in the direction that Simon had gone.

Well, enough of that, Kat couldn't wait to get home now.

Alice babbled in time with the bouncing stroller as Kat raced back to their home. She passed a few people on the way. Were they staring at her? She thought she caught several of them glancing in her direction, but all looked away the moment she returned their gaze.

Eventually she arrived at home. Sergio wasn't there yet. If today went anything like similar days in the past few months, Sergio would come home upset and talk about nearly getting killed by a tractor. They had experienced a day like this every month, around the same time. Could it be the same time?

Before Kat could check the calendar, she heard Sergio open the door. He was home from work early. Just like before.

"Hey love!" Kat said as he walked through the door. "You're back early."

"Yes. And it's the strangest....thing." He broke off. Kat had recognized it too. They had said the exact same words last month. They were reliving a day!

"The tractor?" she asked.

He nodded, "Norma?" he shot back.

Kat also nodded. "We need to figure out what's going on here."

"Agreed. You don't suppose we're in some sort of...I don't know, time loop?"

"Maybe, I don't know how that all works. Though we're not reliving the same month every time. I've noticed some things that are different. Today, for example, I saw something I've never seen before."

And she told him about Norma's red eyes she had seen twice for a brief moment. To her surprise, Sergio didn't seem that surprised. He merely nodded. "Yeah, things have changed for me too. Sometimes just one worker dies by the tractor, sometimes others do too. This time I was prepared and no one got hurt, or tried to hold me down, though several of the workers were looking kind of weird, like they didn't like having me there."

"For me, it's only escalated. I didn't even realize it until Simon touched me, but I remembered all the times that I've talked to him and Norma. Each one was more...heated than the last. I can't imagine what will happen next time."

"If there is a next time. What if we can stop it?"

"How on Earth would we do that?"

Sergio leaned in close. "I suspect those ghosts have something to do with it. Have you ever noticed that on the day that you see Norma, and the day I run afoul of that tractor, it also happens to be the day that Lance goes to fight those ghosts. Every time."

Kat frowned. "That's too much of a coincidence."

"I think so too. Maybe if we put our heads together, we could fight those ghosts and..."

"No, Lance has that covered. I don't want you or me risking our heads again. Alice needs us and we can't afford to endanger ourselves."

"We're already endangered by my estimation."

"So maybe don't go to the granary next time?"

"I tried that today, Tom all but shoved me in the truck and drove me there himself. We're being pushed in a certain direction, I think."

Kat could agree with that. It was the same way she had felt pushed to visit the park today. But now she felt different, ever since Simon had touched her. Was he somehow involved in all this?

Sergio stood, "Well I'm training with Lance tonight, so I've got to be off soon. We have anything to eat?"

"Just some leftovers from yesterday, and there's a box of cereal on the counter."

"Great, I'll have some of that."

He poured himself a bowl of the cereal, added some milk and began chewing down. Kat decided she was a bit hungry herself, so she followed suit.

"Eee," Alice said, understanding that it was time to eat. Kat smiled and began preparing a bottle and some mashed banana.

They ate without talking, with only Alice's babblings to break the silence. Sergio scarfed his food down quickly and began to get ready to leave. It was his turn to train with Lance this week, and he wasn't messing around it seemed.

"What's the big hurry?"

"Oh, I just don't want to be late. Lance wants some help again working on some of his tech. So I'll be a little late coming home tonight."

Kat nodded absently. He had done the same thing last month. Had it even been the same day as the tractor incident? She couldn't remember. Something didn't sit right with her about the explanation, but Sergio had never lied to her before, so...

"You're not going with Lance to fight the ghosts, are you?"

Sergio turned to face her. "Of course not, I'm just making sure his equipment is up to the task. He does all the dangerous work."

"Okay," Kat felt an unexpected wave of emotion pass through her. Her eyes felt moist. "I don't want anything to happen to you."

Seeing the look on her face, Sergio, to his credit, came and wrapped his arms around her. "I'll be fine. We'll figure this out, trust me."

She did trust him. Squeezing him tight, she nuzzled her face in his chest and enjoyed the feeling of his arms around her. Then, he broke the embrace and set off out the door, leaving her alone in the house with Alice. She had a good thing going with Sergio, and he was right. Somehow they would get through this together.

So why did she feel so cold?

CHAPTER 6

"EVERYONE MAKES MISTAKES. SOME HAVE BIGGER
CONSEQUENCES THEN OTHERS."

The most surprising thing about this day, was that nothing unexpected happened.

It was the second Friday of the month, a Friday that both Sergio and Kat had realized was the ominous day when Sergio was chased down by a tractor, and Kat was confronted by Norma in the park. Not to mention the ghosts that Sergio and Lance fought at night, though Kat didn't know Sergio participated in that. At least, he hoped not.

So far, every month, those things had happened on the second Friday of the month, a strange time, but consistent. But so far, today, neither he nor Kat had run afoul of their local enemies. Tom hadn't even asked him to go to the granary and help out. He enjoyed a normal day at work, a warm welcome from Kat at home, a quick dinner, and now he was off to train with Lance for the week, after which he would return to fight the ghosts of Greenfield.

Sergio loved fighting the ghosts, though he hadn't said as much, even to Lance. For the first time since Alice was born, he felt in control of something. Like he was making a difference.

He had given the usual excuse to Kat, that he was going to help Lance tune-up his tech in preparation for fighting the ghosts tonight, promising that he wouldn't do anything else. He didn't enjoy the lie, he had never lied to his wife about anything before. But the thrill of igniting those flamethrowers attached to the iron exosuit...there was nothing like that feeling.

Of course, part of him now wondered if the ghosts would even be there tonight. After a peaceful day so far, perhaps they too were gone. Sergio wouldn't count on it though.

"Ahoy there, Sergio!" Lance called as he entered the abandoned barn where they did their training.

"Hey there, Lance."

"We're pressed for time today, ghost hunting tonight and all. So ready to get started?"

"Oh I am so ready." Sergio grinned. It was the truth.

They started with the standard workout routine Lance had given them for the past month. Sergio was pleased to find he was having less and less difficulty performing the workouts. He was also pleased to see the muscles in his arms and chest swell far larger than he had seen them since...well probably ever. He was practically a new man.

"Not bad, son." Lance still called him son, even though they were the same age. "You're almost there. Only a few more years of this, and you'll be at my level."

"A few years?" Sergio said while panting.

"Yeah, you don't think I learned how to be this fantastic overnight, did you?"

"Certainly not, but—"

"Shut up, son. You're not paying attention. Form's all wrong."

And they continued like that for another hour or two, with Lance making corrections as they went. They were beginning to work on some more aggressive forms now, including some punches and kicks that Sergio found very satisfying.

"Not bad there, Serg. You're learning. Almost as good as your wife."

Sergio grinned, "I've been practicing. Wait...what do you mean, almost—"

But Lance wasn't listening anymore, he was already on his way out the door and headed towards his house. Sergio trotted to keep up.

"Your wife still thinks you're helping me with the mechanisms?" Lance said as Sergio drew closer.

"Yes, which is technically true. I just haven't told her the full story."

"I'd tell her the truth sooner or later, nothing good comes from a lie."

Sergio nodded his head. He knew Lance was right, but he also knew that the moment he told Kat would be the moment that he stopped going with Lance to fight ghosts. And he loved fighting the ghosts.

Lance didn't say another word about it before they arrived at the foothills, in the same clearing as always. Sergio checked the nozzles on his suit to make sure they worked. Small jets of flames shot out each one in a satisfying spurt.

"Okay, I think we're ready," said Lance, checking his own nozzles.

No sooner had he said it when the screams began. Sergio

raised his fists, preparing himself. It wasn't until he saw the first ghost appear in front of him, that he found himself smiling. Time to make short work of these apparitions.

He and Lance were a fighting team. Each one began taking down ghosts left and right. Lance still held an edge on Sergio, but now, in Sergio's third attempt, he was beginning to hold his own. The fire coming out of his hands drew the ghostly figures like moths to a flame, completely mesmerized with the energy, then it only took a few jabs and punches with his iron exosuit before the ghosts were sucked away, through the suit, and into the ground.

Sergio still didn't understand how it all worked. Why, for example, did being redirected into the ground have any effect on the ghosts? Why couldn't they just rise again, immediately? Neither he nor Lance had any explanation, but they knew it worked, at least temporarily, until the next month when the process needed to be repeated.

But that process, as scary as it had been the first time, wasn't all that bad. With the both of them working on it, they managed to mop up the ghosts in record time, only minutes after the screaming started. It wasn't long before he and Lance were looking around in all directions, trying to find any other ghosts. There were none.

"Crumbs, Serg. That wasn't half bad." Lance clapped him on the back. "We'll make a superhero of you yet, even if neither of us actually has superpowers."

"You've proven that one doesn't need superpowers to fight the bad guys, even supernatural bad..." Sergio felt his heart sink as he stared at the trail that they had used to get here.

Kat stood there, with the stroller holding Alice. The look on her face was a mixture of shock and...betrayal. Oh no, this wasn't good.

Sergio quickly extracted himself from the exosuit and went to her. "Kat, I can explain."

"I don't think that's necessary," she said as he approached. Her voice quivered.

"I've been perfectly safe, Lance has been here, I was just helping him out. Think about it as part of my training."

Kat looked from Sergio to Lance. "You knew about this and you didn't tell me?"

"Didn't think it was my place, ma'am, though I did warn Sergio there would be consequences for lying to you."

Thanks for the help, Lance. "It wasn't a lie," Sergio said through gritted teeth. "It just wasn't the whole truth, and I was going to tell you, I promise."

Kat said nothing for a long while. She only held Sergio's gaze, and he did not like what he saw there. For the first time in their marriage, she looked hurt, and because of something he did. It was then that Sergio realized he had been an idiot. What did the thrill of fighting ghosts matter if it hurt Kat? How much would he like playing the hero if she was not beside him?

"Kat, I'm...I'm so sorry. What can I do to..."

A shriek filled the night air. All three of them stopped what they were doing and turned in the direction of the noise. There couldn't be another ghost now, they had finished clearing them out. Lance dove for his exosuit, which he had removed while Sergio and Kat talked. Sergio quickly followed to do the same. But by that time, they could see it.

It was a large one, far bigger than any of the ghosts that Sergio had seen before. It glowed a sickly gray-green, but its most striking feature was its eyes. They glowed a bright red and Sergio could swear he saw intelligence in those eyes. This one was not like the other ghosts.

That thought was confirmed when Lance activated his flames. The ghost glanced in his direction, but didn't freeze or become hypnotized by the firelight. Instead, it rushed at Lance.

"Yaaarrrrggg!" Lance stumbled and fell back, the ghost on top of him. He was pointing the iron spikes of his exosuit into the air, penetrating the form of the red-eyed apparition atop him. But it did nothing. A rhythmic sound came from the ghost. Sergio swallowed. It sounded like...laughter.

Lance screamed again as the ghost touched him. Even in the dim light, Sergio could see Lance's face drain of color. He needed help.

Diving in Lance's direction, Sergio only barely heard his wife protest as he brought his flames to bear. Red eyes met his as he poured fire from the nozzles in his hands.

"Leave him alone!" Sergio yelled with a burst of flame. Lance was shaking now, shivering violently on the ground.

In a split second, the ghost left Lance and appeared instantly at Sergio's side. He tried to pierce it with the iron spikes, but nothing happened. Cold froze his arms and legs, and he too collapsed to the ground. Red eyes stared at Sergio from mere inches away. That was when Sergio knew, he was powerless. He was going to die here tonight.

Alice screamed.

It wasn't a scream of fear, or the kind she gave when she was hungry or stinky. It was a scream of anger, unlike anything Sergio had heard from the girl.

The apparition hesitated. It turned to regard the baby girl with newfound interest. Kat was bending over to take Alice out of the stroller and hold her tight.

Then Lance was at Sergio's side. He brought his iron to bear and swung it through the ghost's form. Sergio, after a moment's hesitation, did the same. The ghost...rippled. That was the only word Sergio knew to describe it. The red eyes moved from Alice, to Lance, to Alice again. The iron wasn't working like it did with the other ghosts, but this time it seemed to be doing something.

The ghost moved fast, leaving Sergio and Lance behind and arriving instantly next to Kat and Alice.

"No!" Sergio yelled. He tried to rise to his feet, but they were feeling weak from the cold left by the ghost. He could barely stand.

Alice screamed again, still in defiance, not in fear or pain.

The ghost took one long look at the girl, then vanished. Silence filled the clearing, broken only by the heavy breathing of Lance, Sergio, and Kat.

Lance crumbled to the ground, clearly in pain.

"Lance, are you okay." Sergio crawled over to check his friend for injuries.

"I..." Lance was shivering. "I....c-can't—" He broke off, saying no more. It looked like he had spent his last remaining strength attacking the red-eyed ghost.

"We need to get him to a hospital," Sergio said.

Kat was closer now, holding Alice in her arms. The baby girl seemed not to realize that something frightening had just happened. Kat took a look at Lance. "There isn't a decent hospital in Greenfield. Just a small clinic."

"Well, then we'll take him there."

"Can we really trust anyone there? After what we've both experienced with the people of this town?"

"Kat, we can't just leave him here. We need to do something!"

Kat nodded, and walked back to the stroller to place Alice in it. "We can take him home. Whatever is wrong, we can help him there."

Sergio wasn't feeling very well himself, but already he had full use of his legs and arms. The ghost obviously had done far less damage to him than it had to Lance.

"Alright, we'll take him there. But if he doesn't improve in the next few hours, we take him to the clinic."

Kat pursed her lips. Sergio could tell she didn't like him insisting right now, especially when she was already mad at him. But finally, she conceded. "Fine, let's get him up."

Together they helped Lance to his feet, and began the slow trek down the foothills and into town. Their home was only about a mile away, but it took much longer for them to reach it, with Lance and a baby stroller in tow. It didn't help that Kat kept shooting fiery glances in Sergio's direction. Yeah, he hadn't heard the end of this. She hadn't said a word since they started walking, but she clearly had not forgotten Sergio's dishonesty.

Finally, they approached and entered their small home. Lance was still shivering as they laid him on their couch.

"I think he has hypothermia," Kat propped some pillows behind Lance's head.

"G-good, deduction," Lance said through chattering teeth. Was he trying to be funny?

"I'll make some tea or something," Sergio chimed in. "Maybe you could get a lukewarm bath running?"

Kat nodded and moved to the bathroom to start the water. They didn't have a huge bath, but it would have to do. Sergio moved to the kitchen to prepare some herbal tea. He didn't wait long for the water to heat. Lance only needed something lukewarm at this point, otherwise the heat would be too much for his body. It wasn't more than slightly-flavored warm water, but it would have to do.

By the time he was done, Kat had reappeared. "The water is ready."

Sergio nodded and gave Lance a sip of the warm water. Lance shivered and sighed with relief. "Oh, that h-hits the s-spot."

"Can you move? We need to help you into the bath."

"Yes, I think so." With help, Lance got to his feet and Sergio guided him into the bathroom. Alice was beginning to cry now, given that her parents hadn't paid her any attention since they entered the house. But neither could spare a moment just yet.

Closing the bathroom door, Sergio helped Lance with his clothes, before gently lowering him into the water. The water wasn't very warm, but Lance still gasped as his feet entered.

"Lie in that for a few minutes then we can raise the temperature." Sergio handed the rest of the tea to Lance who accepted it gratefully.

"W-won't forget th-this," he said, and looked like he meant it.

"I'll be back in a jiffy," he said, and exited the bathroom.

Kat was waiting for him, with arms folded beneath her breasts. "How is he?"

"He's fine, near frozen, but he's already looking better."

"And you?"

Sergio rubbed his arms which still felt tingly. "It didn't get me nearly as bad."

"The point is, it got you. You were taken by surprise tonight."

"Oh come on, Katariina. You know we couldn't have anticipated that. Lance said they behave the same way every month. If he could take care of them alone, why couldn't I help?"

"That's not the issue. The issue is that you lied to me about it."

"Because you would have said no!"

"You're damn right I would have!" Her voice was raised. Alice cried harder now that she continued to be ignored.

"So how can you expect me to ask if you would have said no anyway?"

"You should respect my wishes here."

"Well, you should respect mine!" Sergio was all but shouting now, and it caught Kat off guard. He had never raised his voice at her like that. A few moments of silence, and he took a deep breath. "Look, I'm sorry that I didn't ask you. But you have to understand, I needed this. I loved it."

"I want to leave this place." There were tears in her eyes. "Tonight."

"What? I thought we agreed that we were here for a reason."

"Then we can figure that reason out from outside. I don't want to have to worry about you anymore. First it was the tractor, now this. I...I just." Louder sobs were beginning to emerge, and she slumped against the couch.

Seeing his wife cry, Sergio lost all of his anger in the time it took him to close the distance between them. He cradled her in his arms. "I'm sorry, I'm so sorry. We can try to figure out a way to leave soon, I promise."

Kat didn't respond, but nuzzled her head in his chest, putting her arms around him. He kissed her forehead and wrapped his arms tight around her. He had been a fool. Nothing was more important than Kat, not a thing. Yes, he had his desires, but he needed to respect hers equally, and at the very least talk out their differences.

The embrace didn't last too long, since Alice cranked the volume of her cries up a notch. Kat was about to leave to comfort her, but Sergio put a hand on her shoulder. "I'll take care of her."

He walked to the stroller and picked up his daughter. "Hey there," he said. Alice's cries lessened somewhat, but her face was still red. "Hey, it's okay, we're all here. We're all here."

He ambled around the house, slowly bouncing the girl up and down, feeding, and changing her. He paused only to bring some warmer tea to Lance, who was looking a lot better and managing to add more hot water to the bath on his own.

A few hours later, Alice was falling asleep and Lance emerged from the bathroom, wearing his old clothes. The room was steaming behind him.

"Whew, I never want to go through that again. A moment longer and that red-eyed nightmare would have taken me to their side."

"We're glad you're feeling better." Kat emerged from the kitchen with some more hot tea. Lance accepted it gratefully. "Do you know what it was?"

"Crumbs if I know. Never seen that one before in my life."

"I thought I caught a glimpse of it before, when we first arrived," said Kat. Sergio glanced at her. She had never mentioned that before.

"Well, it must have scampered off because I didn't see it." Lance continued. "I'll need to be more careful in the future." He didn't use the world 'we' implying that he knew, or at least guessed that Sergio was likely not coming with him anymore. There was a long, awkward silence as the seriousness of their predicament set in.

"Listen, uh...I couldn't help but overhear earlier. The two of you are planning to leave?"

Sergio grimaced but nodded. "Yeah, looks that way."

"You can't."

"Lance, I know you need our help and everything, but we need to do what we think is right for our family."

"No, I mean you literally can't. No one has ever left Greenfield. I tried myself a couple of times."

"What do you mean?" Kat's face was full of concern. "Why didn't you say something before?"

"Cause it never came up. You never talked about leaving before. I figured you were sent here and you would figure out why eventually. But here we are, several months in, and still no idea why you're here."

Alice began to cry again, this time from her room. Kat sighed and went to check on her. Sergio turned back to Lance.

"So what exactly does it mean that we can't leave. If we drove off right now..."

And that was when Kat screamed.

Without pausing to think, Sergio acted on instinct and shot towards Alice's room. Inside the door, Kat stood frozen. Sergio pushed past her and saw, for the second time tonight, the red-eyed ghost. It hovered horizontally over Alice's crib, not touching the girl, but observing it mere inches away. It turned to regard them, slowly.

Sergio grabbed the closest object at his disposal, a small lamp, and hurled it at the apparition. It passed right through the ghost, crashing on the wall behind it. The ghost was unaffected, but it seemed to recoil anyway. Before either of them could react further, it had disappeared.

Kat rushed to the crying baby and picked her up, doing her best to calm the child, but looking like she needed calming more than Alice did.

"Sergio, we need to get out of this place, now!" She was not asking, she was demanding. And frankly, no matter what Lance said, Sergio completely agreed.

"You can take my car." They spun to see Lance behind them. "Who knows, maybe you'll make it out. You made it in after all."

He fished in his pockets and produced some keys. Finding the right one, he handed it to Sergio. "Good luck." His face looked solemn, not the usual cheerful, quirky, small-town detective.

"Thank you," Sergio said. He and Kat paused only to grab a few of Alice's diapers and other necessities before they were out the door. They took nothing else. It honestly reminded Sergio of that first night, when they had fled the house with a monster on their tail, held off by a girl they would later learn was their own Alice from the future. This time they were fleeing the house again, but for an entirely different type of monster, one they couldn't even understand.

Sergio tried to breathe easy as they walked hastily to Lance's house to find the car. He almost wished they could be dealing with one of those monsters from Illadar, or wherever they were from. At least they were flesh and blood and could be dealt with as such. This...well this was something stranger.

How had he ever thought it was okay to fight these ghosts, especially when they knew so little about them? How do you fight something you can't understand?

They found Lance's car and got inside. Sergio spun the key in the ignition and the car roared to life. Sergio sighed with relief. When Lance said that they couldn't leave this place, he had half expected the car to not work.

They pulled out of the driveway and Sergio got the car in gear, speeding off towards the nearest highway that cut right through the small town. He turned the car north and began speeding away towards what he believed was San Francisco.

"Thank you for agreeing to this," Kat said from the passenger seat. She was still holding Alice in her arms, not daring to let go of her now. The little girl looked sleepy and wasn't making much noise.

"You were right, I should have never gone with Lance. With this much strange, I should never have assumed I could handle what was thrown at me."

"And I'm sorry that I...stood in the way of what you wanted. I don't want you to think of me as a buzzkill."

"No, but you were right. I should have seen that. It's okay to be a buzzkill when you're more intelligent than me, okay."

She laughed softly, and so did Sergio. He glanced ahead to see the lights of another small town in the distance. Perhaps they would get away after all.

"Besides," he continued, sobering a bit. "Nothing is more important than you and Alice. Nothing. Not even my own desire to be a superhero." That last part sounded silly now that he said it out loud.

Kat chuckled, and Sergio felt her head lean onto his shoulder. "I'll bet you'd look pretty attractive in a cape."

Sergio grinned, "Oh, I'd look amazing."

They laughed again, beginning to feel better as they put more distance between them and Greenfield. They were almost to the next town over when...

"Sergio," Kat's voice had lost its humor. "Isn't that the granary?"

Sergio glanced to the right. It certainly looked like the same granary, but they had passed that going out. "It has to be another one."

"No, look. There's the grocery store up ahead. Did we get turned around?"

"Couldn't have, I've been driving straight down this road the whole time."

But Kat was right, as they entered the town, Sergio recognized each building. They were somehow back in Greenfield.

"Is this what Lance meant when he said we couldn't leave?" Kat was holding Alice tighter than usual.

"Could be. I'm going to keep going and pass through the town on the other side. See if that makes a difference."

But after driving another ten minutes, the same thing happened. They somehow found themselves turned around, and headed back into Greenfield. They tried two more times, always with the same result.

On their last try, the car sputtered and died. Sergio did his best to revive it, but they were stuck once again in Greenfield. Fearing that they would attract the ghost again, they exited the car as quickly as they could and sped towards their street.

"This isn't good, Sergio. How can we be safe if we can't even leave this place."

"I don't know, but I can only think of one solution."

"What's that?"

"We find out what the source of the problem is, and we fix it."

Kat considered that, and didn't say another word until they reached their home. Opening the door, they found Lance still inside, bundled under a few blankets on the couch.

"Crumbs," he said as they entered the door. "I'm sorry, I had hoped it would work. You three have something special about you, and I thought...well it was worth a shot."

Kat strode past Sergio, grabbed a chair from the dining table and set it down in front of Lance. Then sitting, she looked Lance square in the eye. Sergio had rarely seen such a determined look on her face.

"You're going to tell us exactly what's happening. Everything you know. Every observation, every theory, every cock-and-bull idea that has ever entered your brain. Do you get me?"

"Yes, ma'am," said Lance, swallowing. He was wise not to mess with Kat when she was in one of these moods.

Sergio brought over another chair and sat in it. This long night was about to get longer.

CHAPTER 7

"We are in what I call a pocket universe. It's something like a hiccup in time and space." Lance was sitting up, drinking more hot tea that Sergio had brewed. "I'd heard of such things before, though I didn't really put the pieces together until after you three showed up."

"So what exactly is a pocket universe?" Kat probed. "What does it do?"

"Well, each one is slightly different, but from what I gather it creates a sort of time loop until whatever is causing the problem is corrected, which could be tomorrow or it could be never. I heard there was a big one that's been going on since the Renaissance, and the loop consumes whole generations. People die, and are reborn every few hundred years or so to restart the loop. Not sure if anyone's resolved that one yet. Ours is much smaller, but no less dangerous. It only started when the war ended, three years ago, and appears to repeat itself every month."

Sergio was leaning in, fully entranced with the story. "So you're saying, we're repeating the same thing over and over."

"Well, not exactly. See, you've probably noticed that each month doesn't happen *exactly* the same way, just that there are tonal similarities, am I right?"

They nodded, and Sergio asked another question. "But I saw a man die several times, and then he would be back the next month."

"Yes, every month resets the loop, see. People that died are suddenly alive again, with no recollection of what happened to them. But it's not an exact replay of events. That would mean we don't have free will, and there'd be no hope of fixing things. But we do have free will, and that means we have a chance."

"So what are the ghosts?" Kat asked.

Lance shook his head. "I honestly don't know. My best theory is that a pocket universe like this creates an enormous amount of...I don't know, cosmic energy or something like that, and the ghosts are attracted to that. So far, I've only learned how to hold them off, nothing more. And after tonight, that might not be enough."

"What happens if you don't drive them off?"

"They enter the city, and kill everyone inside, like that one almost killed me tonight. Happened once or twice in the beginning. I was the only survivor the first time it happened. But everyone just came back to life the next day, like nothing was wrong. I could see a difference though. They had become...docile. I don't want to know what happens to them when they die and come back to life, but something is lost in the transition."

"We've noticed," Sergio said with a grimace. Kat nodded. There had been something weird about some of the mothers that she met in the park. Sergio had seen the same sort of zombie-like quality among the workers he'd associated with.

"Yes, I suspect there's some larger force at work, but I can't prove it. And until you two came, nothing really changed."

"You think we have something to do with the red eyed ghost?" Kat asked.

"All I know is that there's something about one or more of you that is special, and there's someone that doesn't like it. You've rattled a cage."

Kat glanced at Sergio. They never had told Lance about Alice, about being a future Founder. The question passed silently between them. Sergio shrugged, his way of saying 'go for it.'

"We, ah, haven't told you everything about us. Well, more specifically, we haven't told you everything about Alice."

So she started again from the beginning, telling Lance everything about Invergence and the pursuit that led them here. She didn't leave out anything this time, explaining why Invergence wanted their hands on the little girl. Alice was a future Founder, one of the most important people in Argo Force's organization, and Invergence wanted her for themselves, if for nothing more than to raise her as their own.

"Crumbs," Lance said when she finished. "A Founder! I had no idea. Never thought I'd ever meet one to be honest." He was staring at Alice's room where the girl lay sleeping. "Well, that explains the ghost's interest in her."

"How exactly does it explain that? Alice isn't a Founder yet, and the ghost presumably has no knowledge of her future."

"Presumably, yes. But I suspect there's something more about the girl than meets the eye, see."

"You're saying she has superpowers or something?"

"No, not per se, but there's an...energy that surrounds

people like the Founders. Influencers on a galactica scale, you know. Crumbs, a real Founder." He turned again to stare at Alice's door. "Maybe the ghost detected something in her."

Kat decided to bring the conversation back on topic. "Okay that explains why it's interested in Alice, so how do we drive it off for good, and the rest of the ghosts too? How do we end the loop?"

"Well, I have a few theories, but nothing concrete to go on yet. My guess is that something horribly wrong happened here, or happened to someone here, and that trauma somehow tore a rift in time and space. Either that, or aliens, and I'm inclined to think the former."

"Probably a safe assumption."

"Anyway, if we can find out what happened and somehow correct it, or compensate for it, we may be able to stop the loop. Trouble is, I have no idea where to even start looking."

Kat tapped a finger to her lips. "I may have something. There's a boy I've seen a few times now, Norma's child. I think he might have something to do with this."

"Yes, I've seen the child. What makes you think he's important?"

"I don't know, just a hunch. Norma might also be involved. I saw her eyes flash red the last time we argued. Might even have something to do with the ghost we saw tonight. She seems different from the others, more...assertive. I don't know, it's just a thought."

"Well, we certainly don't have much else to go on." Sergio stood and took Lance's tea cup. "What's our strategy."

"We follow them," Kat said, and both Lance and Sergio turned their heads to look at her. "We need more evidence. Without more information we'll have no idea how to solve the problem, so we start with observation. Then we move on from there."

"Sounds like a plan to me," Lance said cheerfully. "Always enjoyed a good stake out. Though there's only three of us, and I doubt we can keep an eye on Norma and the boy all the time."

"That's okay, we can just start by doing what we can." Kat was feeling a rush of determination. If they were going to fix this, they were going to do it right.

The ghosts had bitten off more than they could chew by threatening Alice.

Unfortunately, following Norma around was easier said than done. For the next few weeks, they did their best to try and find Simon, but the boy was nowhere to be found. On the days that Lance or Sergio watched the home, they could see no sign of the child. Kat hadn't seen him either, not since more than a month past when they had met in the park. She sure hoped nothing had happened to the boy. She wouldn't put it past Norma to hurt him somehow.

Days passed and Kat was growing increasingly frustrated. The real estate agent appeared to be just that. She went to work, showed off some houses to local townspeople interested in upgrading their home, and did nothing else out of the ordinary.

In the end, she, Sergio, and Lance decided that their best shot would be on the second Friday of the month, the day when the number of supernatural oddities seemed to be at their highest.

Kat awoke on that second Friday with an idea. Sergio had already left to join Lance in watching Norma's home. So after giving Alice her morning food and changing her, Kat found herself in the kitchen. She had never been the best cook, but today needed to be different. She rolled up her sleeves, opened up a book on baking, and got to work.

An hour later, she proudly laid out a dozen cookies. They were a little dry, but not all that bad for what Kat was used to. She had followed the recipe to exactness, and it turned out alright. Placing them on a plate, she wrapped it with a foil sheet, and prepared to join her husband and Lance.

Not long after, she pulled the stroller up alongside the car where Lance and Sergio sat. It was parked on the opposite side of the road and further down the street from Norma's house. But it still held a clear view, so if Norma left, they would see it.

"Hey boys," she said as Sergio rolled down the window.

"Careful," Sergio glanced around. "We don't want all three of us to be seen at once, it's risky."

"We agreed that today was the day that we were most likely to learn something. Plus, I had an idea."

Lance spotted, or rather smelled, the cookies in Kat's hand. "Well it was sure nice of you to bring something for us to munch on!"

"These aren't for you," she said absently.

"Say what now?"

Kat sighed, "Look, we haven't seen anything for the past few weeks, which means we need to change up our strategy. And today of all days, I'm not just going to wait around. I made these cookies for Norma, and I'm going to deliver them to her."

"Are you sure that's a wise—"

But Kat was already pushing the stroller ahead. She pulled alongside the house and stopped to take a few deep breaths. The place didn't exactly fit the haunted house vibe, but it was one of those older homes, well...older by Kat's standards, that would be a bit creepy if it weren't in such good condition. Norma obviously liked things to be perfect in her home.

She reached the door, the plate of cookies held in one hand, steeled herself, and knocked.

Someone was definitely home, she heard some sounds from inside. It sounded like Norma was talking to someone, though the sound was too muffled for Kat to make anything of it. Kat waited for a few seconds before she heard a latch at the door. Norma's face appeared through the opening, though she didn't open the door wide enough for Kat to see inside.

"Hi!" Kat said, putting on her most cheerful voice. "Listen, I thought we got on the wrong foot the other day, and I've been feeling so badly about it ever since. I wanted to make it up to you." She offered the plate of cookies.

Norma paused considering what to do, before that fake smile touched her lips. "Very kind of you, dearie. A nice gesture, if somewhat late in arriving."

Kat forced herself to keep smiling. "Are you busy? I thought I heard voices inside."

Norma's eyes flashed, though not with red this time. "Oh, that's just my cat."

"Well, I was hoping maybe I could come in for a bit, maybe we could talk and try to patch things up. Resolve our misunderstandings."

Norma grew more stern. "I'm afraid not, dearie. I've got to go meet with a client about a house. I'm sure you'll understand."

Kat felt her heart sink. This was getting her nowhere. She couldn't see anything inside the house, and Norma was giving her nothing to go on. Should she try to push further?

Maybe they could get a glimpse inside once Norma left. They had never tried to get in the house before, but this time they had a guarantee that Norma would be gone for a while. Yes, that was a good plan. Kat kept the smile on her face. "Of course, I'm sorry to disturb you. Another time perhaps."

"Yes, that would be lovely. You'll understand that today is a very busy day for me."

"Yes, naturally. Perhaps we'll see each other around."

She handed the cookies to Norma, who promptly shut the door in her face. Kat didn't walk back to Sergio and Lance in their car, in case Norma was watching. Instead, she pushed the stroller in the opposite direction until she turned around a corner out of sight. Alice was beginning to babble, saying a few words, naming the familiar objects around her. She had been unexpectedly quiet while they were at Norma's door.

She peeked around the corner, hoping that none of the neighbors were watching too closely. After a few moments, Norma exited her house, locked it, and left in a small automobile. As Kat had guessed, she was driving towards the row of new houses that Kat and Sergio lived on, the opposite direction from Kat's hiding place.

Once she was sure that Norma really was gone, she turned around and walked the stroller back down the street, eventually arriving at Lance's car. Sergio rolled down the window.

"Did you learn anything?" he asked eagerly.

"Not much. She didn't open her door all the way. Though I swear I could hear voices before she answered the door. She claimed she was talking to her cat, but I'm not so sure."

"You think there could be someone still in the house?"

"I think we should check to find out."

"What?" said Lance. "Just go inside her house? That's breaking and entering."

Kat rolled her eyes, "I think the circumstances justify that much at least."

Lance looked like he was about to say something, then he closed his mouth and remained quiet. Sergio grabbed Kat's hands. "What if it's not Simon in there? What if Norma has some sort of co-conspirator, or someone dangerous inside?"

"If you want to protect me, you can come with me. But I'm going into that house, one way or another."

Sergio pursed his lips, but reached a decision. Unbuckling, he exited the car. Lance followed suit right behind.

"Okay," said Sergio as he stood. "We're really doing this."

"There's no better day to try," said Kat. "It's the second Friday of the month, if we don't learn something today, we'll have to wait even longer, and who knows what could happen in that time."

Both Sergio and Lance seemed to be onboard by now, so Kat led them back to Norma's home. She knocked, and listened hard. Was that a rustling she heard? She tried the handle, but it was locked. So she turned around and began walking to the back of the house.

"Can't believe we're doing this in broad daylight." Lance glanced around nervously. "What if someone sees us?"

"It can't be worse than what that ghost did to you." Kat pointed out.

Lance considered that and eventually shrugged. "Crumbs, if my mother could see me now."

Kat didn't bother to consider what his mother would do. Instead, she located the back door and gave it a small shove. Nothing. Darn, maybe she could...

This time she definitely heard it, a muffled sound coming from inside. It was coming from one of the basement windows at the base of the house. Getting on her knees, she crouched down and shielded her vision to try and get a glimpse of what was in the dark room.

She could make out something. A small form on a chair, though the darkness made it difficult to see any details. The muffled sound came again. There was definitely someone in there. Could it be Simon?

The window was one of those permanent fixtures, so she couldn't open it. But by now, she had lost all sense of stealth. She would get in the house if she had to break down the door to do it. Standing up from looking in the window, she faced Lance. "Can you get in the door?"

Lance rubbed the back of his neck. "I...um, I'm not sure that's wise."

"There is someone in the basement, someone small. I think it's Simon and I think he might be in trouble. We need to get in there, now!" Her tone did not inspire argument. Lance fished in his pockets and brought out a few metal sticks, obviously made for lock picking. "The guys at the office would not like me having these, but I figured it was a good skill to have."

He walked up to the back door while Kat and Sergio watched, enraptured. It took a while, longer than Kat felt comfortable waiting. Lance told them several times that they needed to be patient, that unlocking a door took precision. Kat was about to question Lance's skill at lock picking when finally, something caught and the door swung open.

"There, see. I told you I'd get it eventually," Lance said.

Kat didn't have the heart to tell him that most doors didn't take twenty minutes to unlock for a professional. But she lost that thought as soon as she entered. It took only seconds to locate the door to the basement.

She readied herself for what she might find there and stepped down the stairs. Unfortunately, her fears were completely founded. Tied to a chair, in the middle of the room was Simon. The boy's face was pale and he had tears in his eyes. His head remained slumped to one side, but his eyes were open, and they found Kat's.

"Oh my goodness, Simon." She rushed to him, finding the cords that held his hands to the armrests of the chair. "What has she been doing to you?"

"Hurts," was all Simon could manage.

"Something fishy is definitely going on here," Lance said as he looked from the boy to the rest of the house.

"Yeah," said Sergio. "I've noticed it too. There's hardly anything in this house. Norma must be some minimalist."

"Or, her needs are not the same as ours." Lance speculated.

"Will you two shut up and help me free this boy?" Kat was trying and failing to undo the cords tying Simon.

"Oh yes, of course." Lance produced a small pocket knife from his pocket. The man sure made a good Boy Scout. He seemed prepared for everything.

Lance used the knife to slice cleanly through the cords. Simon took his hands and lifted them, as if disbelieving that he was really free.

Then he shot to his feet faster than Kat would have thought possible for a boy in his condition. He had seemed so weak a moment before.

"Go!" He indicated the door, taking a few steps himself.

Kat felt no need to argue. They had the boy, and there

was no way she was going to let Norma have him again. They needed to get out.

They climbed the stairs and emerged into the kitchen and dining room above. The others had been right, Kat realized. There was nothing here. A few candy wrappers littered the floor. Had Norma been feeding Simon only candy? There was no fridge, nothing to indicate there was extra food in the house. Though Kat's cookies lay untouched on the counter.

"I knew you couldn't possibly be here because you felt sorry."

The three of them whirled to face the speaker, and Kat felt a familiar fight or flight sensation take over her body. She hadn't felt that since they first arrived in Greenfield. It was Norma, hands on hips, smiling and looking like she had just caught someone digging into the cookie jar. Simon stood behind Kat, and she could feel him shivering. She just wasn't sure if it was the cold from being stranded in the basement for so long, or fear of Norma.

"Well, well, well. What have I caught?"

Lance was the first to make a move. He stepped forward, producing a badge from his jacket. "I'm afraid it's not us who are caught, ma'am. We've seen this here abuse of your child and I simply will not stand for it. You're under arrest."

Norma's smile widened, unnerving Kat even more, which she had not thought possible. "Oh, I don't think so, young man. I am this town, all are under my control."

"Not all," Kat said, trying to keep a brave face, but still fighting that unexplainable dread that threatened to overtake her.

Norma faced her. "All," she emphasised the word. "But go ahead, take the boy. He means very little to me now anyway."

"What kind of a monster are you?" Sergio was staring at the woman. "What kind of mother keeps her son locked up, starved and without anyone to love him?"

Lance produced a pair of handcuffs from his belt, and cautiously approached the woman. Norma regarded him without fear. Staring from him to the others.

"What kind of monster am I? I think you already have an idea."

Kat swallowed. Norma was right. She did have an idea. And she had been hoping until now that she was wrong.

Norma's eyes flashed a fiery red, and then the rest of her began to change. Lance jumped back as Norma turned translucent, her hair darkened, and her eyes glowed even brighter. There was no mistaking it. Norma was the red-eyed ghost from the foothills.

Simon screamed. It was far greater volume than Kat would have expected from him, weak as he was. Alice began to cry.

A terrible laughter filled the room. Like multiple voices laughing in unison. Some a deep rumble, others a high-pitched cackle.

"Still think you're in charge here?" The voice came from Norma, now in full ghost form. "I could kill all of you without a thought."

"So why don't you?" Kat said, sounding braver than she felt. She was clutching Alice so hard, the girl was squirming.

The ghost looked...thoughtful, if that was an expression ghosts were capable of. "I may have uses for you. Go ahead and take the boy. He's served me as much as I needed."

"I won't let you ever lay a finger on him again," Kat growled.

"Oh I very much doubt that...dearie." Norma said the last word with what looked like a smile.

And with a loud rush of air, she was gone.

Kat found that all three of them were breathing heavily, Alice was crying, and Simon looked like he was about to hyperventilate. It was Sergio who broke the silence.

"Do you...do you think that she's right? Are we really as powerless as that...whatever that was, suggests?"

"Son, no enemy has ever admitted his weaknesses before today, and I don't expect that to change, even from a ghost. She has a weakness or I'm a gopher." The detective seemed decidedly calm for having just met the ghost that nearly killed him a few weeks earlier. He could have been talking about the weather.

"But the way she just let us take the boy..."

"I think she was telling the truth," Kat interjected. "At least in part. I think she really doesn't care about the boy anymore. Before, when I confronted her about Simon, she got all upset. I didn't see any of that this time."

Sergio leaned close and spoke in a low voice to keep Simon from hearing. "Yeah, about that. What are we going to do with him? Take him in ourselves?"

Kat nodded. "At least until we figure this out. He's the only lead we have on what's going on here. He might help us learn something. Besides, would you trust anyone else with him, in this town?"

Sergio shook his head. "Not a one. Okay then, let's get him home. He looks half starved, and the other half frozen."

"I'll see what I can dig up about these two in our archives," said Lance, rubbing his stubble. "I know the station has a few records, and I know a few others places I could check. Should at least be able to find the boy's birth certificate and other such documents."

Kat turned to the boy, who still shook in terror. "Simon. We're going to let you come to our house for a little bit. You can play with Alice and we'll make sure you have a lot of good food and a warm place to sleep. Would you like that?"

Simon nodded vigorously. "Yes, please."

Kat smiled. "Well, it's decided then! Alice would love to have a friend." Alice picked the perfect time to coo.

They left Norma's house out the back door and returned to the car. They all piled in, filling the vehicle.

That night, Kat found herself unable to sleep. She was acutely aware of the creaks and groans in the house. Each one made her want to prop herself up and look at Simon and Alice, who slept in the same room now, so they could keep a close eye on them.

Kat still had no idea how they were going to handle this situation. How could you fight ghosts? Truly fight them. Was it even possible? And what did Simon have to do with it?

These questions kept her up all night. What she didn't notice was that she wasn't the only one watching Simon. A pale red light kept appearing from time to time outside the window, unbeknownst to all.

CHAPTER 8

"OH I LOVE IT WHEN A LOT OF STUFF IS EXPLAINED. SOME
OF IT AT LEAST. WE CAN'T GIVE AWAY TOO MUCH JUST YET."

L ance slammed something heavy on the table, causing Sergio to jump out of his power nap with a start.

"I think I've found the answers, see," said Lance, his eyes wide with excitement. "Picked these up from old Granny Jumpers about two streets over.

Sergio blinked the sleep away from his eyes and finally realized what was in the box. It was stuffed full of newspapers, from several outlets by the look of things.

They had been trying to do some research on Simon or Norma's past, anything that could give them an edge in their little Ghostbusters problem. Greenfield was too small to have a library, or even a local newspaper. And being unable to leave the city meant that they couldn't do any extended research. But Lance's police station had a few things, and that's where they were now. Lance had brought Sergio in as a "research assistant" for an old "cold case" he was looking into. At least that's what they told the rest of the officers. But so far, they had found nothing. Now Sergio sat staring at a bunch of new newspapers with renewed interest.

"This first one is marked January of nineteen forty-six." He picked up the paper in question. "Just a few months after the war."

"That's right, and there are some even further back, right up to the end of the war itself."

"This is exactly what we're looking for, who did you say gave you these?"

"Old Granny Jumpers. Apparently she gets deliveries from several newspapers in the area. Said she didn't trust getting her news from just one source. I asked if I could take the first few years' worth beginning in nineteen forty-five and she was hesitant but I eventually persuaded her. Seems like not all of the city's residents are Norma's minions."

Sergio glanced around. "Which reminds me, I've been getting a lot of dirty looks from the cops here, for no good reason. Maybe we should look through these back at the house."

"Excellent idea, chap." Lance was in surprisingly good spirits. "Let's get cracking."

Lance carried the box to his car, and Sergio joined him, avoiding the stares of Lance's co-workers on his way out. They said nothing, but Sergio couldn't shake the uneasy feeling they gave him. Normally, he would have chalked it up to some racial divides, but in this town, he wasn't sure that was the only reason.

They soon arrived at the house, and Sergio went to open the door for Lance, who carried the box inside.

Kat was there, holding Alice. She held the girl a lot more these days, ever since she had seen Norma's ghost approach the girl. And since they had taken Simon, a lot of strange things had been happening around the house. Locks that opened, objects that seemed to move when you weren't looking. It creeped Sergio out, and Kat was even more worried.

Simon emerged from the bedroom to see who was here, and his face lit up when he saw Sergio and Lance. The boy had taken an extreme liking to the detective ever since he stood up to Norma.

"Hey there, champ!" said Lance as he set his box of newspapers on the dining table. "You're looking better every time I see you."

Which was true, Sergio realized. The boy had put on a lot of weight since they started feeding him properly. They had learned that Norma hardly ever fed the boy, and when she did, it was usually candy or other sweets. Apparently that's what Norma thought kids liked, so it was all he got. It made Sergio shiver. It was like something right out of Hansel and Gretel.

"What's that?" Kat indicated the box of newspapers on the table.

"More research!" Lance beamed as if research was the world's best pastime. "I have a good feeling about this lot."

Sergio explained where they had gotten the newspapers and when they were from. Kat's eyes widened. "Well, we should get to work."

She put Alice down in her playpen, making sure that it was right next to the table, to watch the girl closely. Alice didn't really like the playpen anymore; it was too confining for her. But it was less confining than her mother's arms, so she only pouted instead of cried.

They set to work sorting the papers by date, then by outlet. Then each of them took a separate outlet and began to read. It was long work, as they tried to read carefully for any clue, anything to help them out.

Sergio was the first to find something. He almost

skipped right over it. "Hey guys, look, it's an obituary for Norma!"

"What?" Kat asked. "But she's still alive. Couldn't it be another Norma?"

"No, this is definitely her. 'Norma Weathers, real estate agent, from Greenfield, California. Died, January twelfth, nineteen forty-six.' Wow, Simon would only have been two or three at the time."

"Keep reading," Kat said, intrigued.

"Let's see, 'She is survived by her young son Simon, and her brother-in-law...Trevor Weathers, who will take care of the child until he comes of age.'" Sergio looked up. "I never knew Trevor was related. And he's the one who died multiple times at the granary. That can't be a coincidence."

"Good deduction, son," said Lance. "I agree. Perhaps if we continue searching, we'll find more."

So they descended into studious silence again, broken only by Alice's laughter nearby. Simon had gone to her, and was sticking his fingers into the mesh of the playpen and wiggling them, which Alice somehow thought was extremely funny.

But they hadn't studied long before Kat suddenly jumped to her feet. Sergio and Lance jumped too, startled by the sudden movement. "I've got it." Kat breathed heavily. "I know why all of this is happening."

And she proceeded to read the article.

Local Boy, Orphaned and Homeless, Saved by a Miracle

Simon Weathers, a boy from Greenfield, California, was the victim of several unfortunate events from a very young age. His father never returned from the beaches of France, and his mother seemingly died after wandering off into the foothills when the boy was only three years old.

While her body was never found, she was presumed dead when an unidentifiable corpse was found at the base of a cliff.

Following the tragic accident of his parents, Simon passed to Trevor, his uncle, who barely cared for the boy, and frequently left him alone at home while he went to work.

While the boy had no knowledge of safety precautions, he would often leave the house, where local authorities would find him, often in the town's centrally located park, a favorite destination of Simon's. Sadly, the boy gained little sympathy from these men, who considered him more of a curiosity than a victim, according to onlookers at the park. None of these officers could be found for questioning.

One sad night, the boy wandered even farther from home, finally arriving in the foothills outside of town. There, lacking food and water, he collapsed from utter exhaustion, and would have died had it not been for what some are calling a true modern miracle.

It was in that state of near-death that Simon's mother found him. Yes, you read that correctly. Simon's mother miraculously returned from the grave, or it would seem, had never entered the grave to begin with. Whether by fate or motherly intuition, she located her son and brought him home to be nourished and cared for once again.

Kat stopped there and looked up at Lance and Sergio. "The foothills, Trevor, the park. These are all connected."

Sergio nodded. "Well, I think that confirms the theory that the boy has something to do with all the strange things happening in this town."

Lance was fingering his chin. "I seem to remember some of my mates talking about a boy in the park. But I never realized that he was completely alone. They kept referring to him as 'Trevor's boy' so I naturally assumed Trevor was with him."

"So what exactly happened here." Sergio placed his hands flat on the table. "I think it's safe to assume that the return of his mother was actually the apparition, and not his real mother."

Lance nodded. "Yes, my guess is that Simon's suffering in those foothills opened the breach there. And I'd wager all my gears and bobbles that the boy was there on the second Friday of the month. It all adds up."

"Yes, but why Simon?" Kat asked. "I mean, this is a horrible situation to have lived through, but let's face it, worse things have happened. Why did this tear a breach in the universe, and not other horrible experiences?"

"Who knows?" Lance shook his head. "There are a lot of variables involved in the causation of such supernatural events. Perhaps he has a special destiny ahead of him. Fate can be a powerful force, even before a child grows into their destiny. Like I said before with your Alice. Or, it could be that other things have happened in this area, perhaps thousands of years ago, to weaken the barrier between this world and the next. And Simon's experience could have been the last straw that tore a hole in the universe. We probably will never know."

"Lance," Sergio asked a question that had been on his mind for a while. "Just where did you learn all this stuff?"

Lance shuffled his feet. "Erm, here and there."

Sergio didn't like that answer. Lance was obviously hiding something, but now wasn't the time to push further. He leaned back in his chair. "Okay, if the boy somehow caused the breach, can he seal it? There's got to be a connection there somehow. I think...hey, where did Simon go?"

They looked around. Simon was not next to Alice's playpen anymore. He couldn't have left through the door. Someone would have seen him. Kat rose to her feet so fast her chair fell over behind her. Then she ran to the bedroom door. Sergio was right on her heels, though Lance went to another corner of the room, checking up on his ghost-hunter equipment he kept there. Probably to make sure it was all there.

Once inside the bedroom, Sergio immediately noticed that the window was open. He swore under his breath, but Kat had already swung around. She pushed past him, covered the length of the room in a flash, and launched herself out the front door. "Simon!" she yelled. "Simon, it's okay."

Sergio peered out the window to see that the boy hadn't got far. He was only partway down the road, and Kat had already closed the distance between them by half. Sergio breathed a sigh of relief as his wife caught up with the boy. Well, the newspaper had said that he was prone to leave the house and wander.

Sergio turned to go back into the living room. A quick glance out the window on his way out told him that Kat had the boy and was bringing him back. Sergio looked at Lance. "Everything accounted for?" he asked. Lance nodded.

The front door opened and Kat and Simon walked in. The boy held his arms tight with his hands, clearly scared. Kat gently encouraged him with a soft push to enter the room, which Simon did reluctantly.

Sergio knelt to be on the boy's level. "Hey Simon, it's alright. We aren't going to hurt you. We're here to protect you, to make sure that scary lady doesn't lay another finger on you."

"Hurt." The boy repeated back.

"Yes, we won't' let anyone hurt you."

Simon shook his head. Then he pointed at Alice, then at Kat, and finally Sergio. "Hurt," he said again.

"You think Norma will hurt us?" Sergio clarified. The boy nodded. A tear started down one eye, and Simon brushed it away with his fist.

Sergio's heart melted, and he took Simon into his arms. "Oh, my boy. You're going to be just fine. Thank you for caring what happens to us. That means you're a very good boy. And don't worry, we have things that will help keep the ghost away. She won't hurt us." He wasn't so sure about that, but the boy needed comfort right now, not the uncertain truth.

Simon shook his head. "Momma hurt, Momma hurt!" His voice grew frantic, higher in pitch. "Momma hurt!"

"Yes, Momma will hurt. Just not yet, dearie." A voice called out. Sergio leapt to his feet, letting go of Simon. He couldn't see anything, no ghostly figure. Just the disembodied voice.

Kat was the first one to work up the courage to speak out loud. "We've done fairly well so far. We dismantle your minions each month."

A cold laugh sounded through the house. "You know nothing about power, little girl. You stand idly by while it watches you, while it hides behind your very nose."

"So show yourself. Prove your power."

The laugh sounded again. As it did, the sound grew clearer, as if emerging from underwater, or behind a door. Sergio steeled himself for what came next.

First came the eyes, red as Mars, illuminating all of

them. A pale form followed, filling the entire end of their living room, tendrils of hair and cloth floating in all directions. It was Norma, in her most dangerous ghostly form. It was all Sergio could do to keep from cowering. And a glance at Kat told him she probably felt the same. Her eyes were locked on the demon, opened wide. Sergio couldn't see what Lance was doing behind him, but he assumed the detective also fixed his stare on the ghost.

Simon and Alice screamed at the same time, and the boy fell backward, knocking his head on the back of a chair and collapsing to the floor. Sergio bent to check on him. He was out cold, and his head was bleeding. Sergio checked Simon's pupils and pulse. Everything else seemed alright. He would have a huge headache when he awoke, but that was it. The image of the ghost shivered in delight, almost looking like it was taking a deep breath of fresh air.

"Look at you!" The spectral image said. "You tremble at my presence. And rightly so. I revel in your fear, it gives me power over you!"

"If you're as powerful as you claim, why haven't you killed us by now? We've been here, plotting your demise. Why let us?" Kat looked less fearful now, turning away from Simon. Instead she...studied the ghost. She was genuinely curious.

"Because there is nothing you can do."

"Nothing? That's an extreme word. You've been trying to get rid of us from the moment we arrived. But now you're keeping us here, and you're not trying to kill us. Why?"

"None can leave Greenfield."

"Yeah, but you could change that, right? Why not just let us go."

The ghost stood still.

"Unless..." Kat looked like she had an idea. "Unless you

can't leave either. You're trapped here just like us, aren't you?"

A hiss escaped the apparition. "You know nothing of what you speak. Soon I will have enough power to leave this place."

"Then why are you even here, right now. Did we do something to offend you, oh mighty ghost lady?"

The red eyes flashed. "You mock me!" Sergio almost put a hand on Kat's shoulder to stop her. She was beginning to take things a little too far.

"I wish only to understand you."

"Then understand this." The image of Norma swelled until it nearly filled the whole room. "I am not some petty villain that you can order about so. I am pure light from the beyond. I am the soul of countless dead. I am legion!"

Kat didn't seem to catch the Biblical reference, but Sergio did. He swallowed, wondering not for the first time, if they were in over their heads.

"Why did you leave us the boy?" Kat stood unimpressed, her hands on her hips. She really was determined to get something out of the ghost. Sergio glanced back at Lance, who was fiddling with something as nonchalantly as he could. The ghost didn't seem to notice.

"He was of no use to me."

"Then I ask again. Why are you bothering us?"

The ghost paused, caught in an internal dilemma. Then its eyes flashed again. "You dare to question me?"

Kat smiled. "I've hit upon something, haven't I?"

The house shook. Alice screamed again and Sergio bent to grab the table for support. Kat stumbled but remained upright.

"YOU WILL COME TO KNOW MY POWER!" Norma's voice filled their ears, louder than they had ever heard before.

Sergio covered his own ears, but saw light fill the room. That was when he noticed other apparitions, appearing on all sides. A dozen of them at least. They were gathering around Norma, peering down at them from the ceiling.

Sergio swallowed. It appears they *were* in over their heads. Kat had also seen the newcomers, and for once had nothing to say. Why had she antagonized the ghost lady?

Suddenly, Lance pushed past Sergio and cleared the distance between him and Norma's ghost. He was wearing his iron exosuit used to take out ghosts. What was he thinking? The exosuit hadn't worked on Norma before; there was no reason to think now would be any different.

Lance didn't even bother with the flames, instead he simply jabbed the iron spike into the ghostly image.

And Norma screamed.

Instead of passing straight through the ghost, like Sergio had expected, the iron spike lodged there, as if penetrating the ghost, much as the spike would have penetrated and hurt a human. A pale smoke began to ooze from the wound as Lance plunged it deeper, twisting as he went.

Norma screamed again, a piercing sound that radiated all around them. The other ghosts took up the cry and held their heads as if they too were in pain.

Then they began to disappear.

One by one, each ghost left the house, screaming as they went. Norma was the last to go, staring at Lance, then beyond to where Kat and Sergio stood. She looked at them, as if seeing them for the first time. Then she too was gone, vanishing into mist.

The house was left in a silence that Sergio could not have imagined a moment earlier. Nothing moved. Nothing made a sound.

"What did you just do?" Kat said to Lance.

"I..uh. I can't believe that worked." Lance looked like he hadn't heard Kat.

"You can't believe what worked?" Sergio echoed Kat's question.

"The boy's blood. It was just a hunch, but I had the nagging feeling that it would somehow weaken the apparition."

Sergio glanced down at Simon, who was still unconscious and a small trickle of blood came from one side. Kat bent down to pick the child up and carry him to the bed. Sergio followed. They both momentarily forgot about Lance's revelation while they checked to make sure Simon was alright. Sergio propped his feet up then went into the kitchen to make some hot chocolate. The boy would probably want something warm and sugary when he awoke.

When he returned, Kat was rubbing the boy's forehead with a damp cloth. The blood had been washed clean, and Simon wasn't bleeding anymore, which was a good sign. Apparently the cut hadn't been that deep. Still, anyone who got knocked out likely had a small concussion at the very least.

"How's he doing?" Sergio asked.

"He's fine, he's starting to stir."

Lance was standing nearby, watching. Sergio turned to him. "So you're saying you took some of the boy's blood and...coated the iron bar with it? How'd you know that would work?"

"I honestly didn't, see. The thought just came to me. I thought, if the boy was necessary to close the breach, like we determined, then maybe he could be used as a weapon. And blood has some magical properties, or so I've been told. I figured it was worth a shot, especially with your wife keeping the ghost's attention like she was."

Again, Sergio wondered where Lance had learned everything he knew, but he shrugged it off. The boy was blinking and beginning to move.

"W-where?" He began to panic as he came to, looking everywhere for the ghost of his so-called mother.

"Shh, everything is fine, Simon." Kat placed her hands firmly on Simon's shoulders, helping him lie back down. "The ghost isn't going to bother you tonight. We took care of her."

The boy looked at her, incredulous. "How?"

"Well, you know Lance? He took a little of your blood and used it to hurt her. She ran away."

The boy stared at Lance like he would look at a superhero. "Wow," he said eventually.

Sergio chuckled and sat on the edge of the bed. "Yes, you see. We won't let the scary lady hurt you. You're safe with us."

Simon leapt up and flung his arms around Sergio, who sat taken aback. Eventually he put his arms around the boy. "It's okay."

Kat joined them, wrapping her arms around the pair. "We love you, Simon. You have a place with us."

Sergio felt cold metal as Lance, still in his exosuit, also joined the group hug. He didn't say anything, but the four of them held that position for a long time. It was a moment Sergio would remember.

A while later, Simon was sleeping and Kat and Sergio were in the living room, playing with Alice. The girl was really starting to talk now, saying words like 'more, fly, car,' and a variety of animal names, even though they had no animals with them at the moment. Tonight, however, they heard a new one: 'ghost,' which she would say with her hands up and her teeth bared, like a normal child might say 'roar'.

That sobered them up a bit. Alice was going to have an upbringing that was far different than most young children experienced.

Lance continued fiddling with his exosuit for a few more hours, spreading the blood more evenly around the spike and using some oil to keep it from drying and flaking off.

"I think we might consider taking shifts through the night," he said when he was done. "That woman might come back when we least expect it, and right now this is the only weapon we have against her and the other ghosts. We should have someone ready to use it."

Sergio and Kat agreed, so they kept a lookout for the rest of the night. Lance also stayed the night, and slept on the couch in the living room. Sergio took the first watch. He stayed in the master bedroom, looking at Kat, Simon, and his daughter as they slept peacefully. The night passed without incident, and eventually he awoke Lance for the next watch. Then he put his head down and entered a restless sleep, pitted with nightmares.

CHAPTER 9

"I THINK I CAN STILL REMEMBER THIS PART, VAGUELY. I DON'T THINK I LIKED IT."

Sergio was beginning to believe that the ghosts were no longer a concern, that they had frightened them off for good. He didn't really think that of course, but they had seen nothing from Norma or any ghost in the past few weeks. Lance seemed to think that the second Friday of the month was sort of focal point, when the ghosts were strongest. Since they had wounded Norma on the last second Friday of the month, the theory was that she had retreated to recharge.

But the day was back again, now in the month of September. It seemed crazy to Sergio that so much time had already passed since they first arrived in Greenfield. It was almost like that fog over his mind was still there, at least in traces, muddling time.

Lance was over again. He spent most of his days at their house now, where they could guard each other's backs. They had kept a watch ever since last month, but had seen nothing. Now, Lance brought his two exosuits, and a third one he was working on for Kat. He'd made some adjustments to the suit and was now explaining to both of them.

"I've coated all the spikes with a combination of Simon's blood, some oils, and a form of resin. That should keep the blood from fully drying, but still keep it attached to the spike. I've also added a few holes in the resin here, and here." He indicated points along the spike. "So that the basic use of the iron still works. If all goes well, it should still suck them into the iron."

"But then they're just transferred into the ground like before. What good does that do us?" Sergio asked. He had a good point. They couldn't just keep playing cleanup each time the ghosts arrived. They needed a more offensive tactic.

"Ah, I had a thought about that. You ever heard two microphones when they get close to each other?"

They both nodded. "Of course," Kat said. "It creates a feedback loop that creates a high-pitched noise and increases in volume."

"Well, I thought maybe I could do something of that sort with the electrical feedback of this device. The ghosts are energy after all."

Sergio peered closer to the modifications in Lance's exosuits. "You've created an electrical feedback loop. It no longer feeds them into the ground."

Lance beamed. "Yup. My theory is, if they are injured by Simon's blood, it might weaken them so that once caught in a feedback loop, it will overload their ghostly...um, visage, and they'll die out in the loop. Course, the drawback is that the iron in this part of the exosuit," he indicated a section along the back, "will probably grow quite hot, so I've done what I can to insulate it."

"That sounds...actually quite scientific." Sergio sat back, impressed. "Are you sure science will have any effect on ghosts?"

"Son, everything is science, even ghosts. We're just still learning how the science works."

"That's a lot like what Arthur C. Clarke said, 'Any sufficiently advanced technology is indistinguishable from magic.'"

"Who is Arthur C. Clarke?"

Sergio hesitated, "He's an author. He's probably not famous yet."

"Anyway," Lance went on. "I'm hoping to test these tonight, in the foothills."

"We're still doing that?" Kat interjected. She was feeding Alice at the table and didn't look too pleased with the conversation.

"Urm, yes. I mean, if they come back, which they always have, someone will need to be there, to keep them from coming into the city." Lance looked uncomfortable. He always looked that way whenever Kat was displeased.

"And besides, we have a chance of dispatching these ghosts permanently this time," Sergio added. "We can't let that chance slide."

Kat clearly didn't like it, but she also didn't argue. "Okay, but you need to get that third exosuit in working condition so I can use it. Someone has to stay home with Simon and Alice to protect them."

"Right you are, ma'am. I'll get to work on that right away."

As Lance bent over the equipment, Simon came bursting into the room, looking for once like he was happy. He peered at what Lance was doing, eager to see what was happening. Once they had explained the situation to Simon, he had generously agreed to donate some more of his blood, and didn't even cry when they stuck him with a needle to extract it. Now, he was a few pounds heavier, and in far better spirits than he had been the last two months.

"Hey there, champ," Kat said as he bounded across the room.

He looked at the mashed banana that she was feeding Alice. "Please, may I have some food?"

He was so polite that both Sergio and Kat laughed. "Of course you can have some. Give me a moment." Kat stood and went to the kitchen to grab another banana. That was most of what she fed the kids these days. Fresh fruit and vegetables. It meant she didn't have to cook. Simon didn't complain; he seemed genuinely happen to have something to eat. And Alice, well she didn't always like it, but didn't really have a choice.

Armed with a banana and an apple, Simon sat at the table and began to peel.

"Did you hear us talking earlier?" said Sergio. "Lance and I are going to take care of those ghosts, once and for all, so they can't bother us again."

Simon's face fell, almost instantly, which was not the reaction Sergio expected. "Don't fight them. Don't go," he said.

"Why not?" Sergio seemed genuinely confused. Lance too looked up from his work, brows furrowed.

"Bad things happen." Simon had disregarded his food.

"But we're better prepared this time. Remember what Lance did to your mother's ghost the last time? We're going to do that again, but to all of the ghosts."

"Bad things happen," Simon repeated.

They tried for a while to get him to say more, but Simon had turned inward, as he often used to do. It had been a while, and Sergio had begun to think the boy was getting over his trauma. But he guessed one certainly didn't get over such things too easily. His wife still hasn't recovered from seeing that family die at the hands of Invergence. How was one supposed to move on from such things?

"This worries me, Sergio," Kat told him later. "He seems really upset about you going to the foothills tonight."

"Well, it's not as though we have a choice. Lance has been doing this for a long time. I think we'll be okay, especially with this new stuff made from Simon's blood. If that doesn't work..."

"That's what I'm afraid of. We don't have much of a guarantee that it will work."

Sergio pulled her close and kissed her forehead. "We'll be fine. I promise to run if anything happens. We'll get out of there."

"Thank you," Kat said. She stayed silent for a while, clearly thinking hard about the situation they were in. But ultimately, she had agreed to the necessity of what Lance and Sergio did to defend against the ghosts.

Lance left an exosuit for Kat to use, which she took gratefully, albeit hesitantly. Then Lance spent an hour or so training them on the use of the suit's new features. For Sergio, there wasn't much new to learn, but he appreciated the refresher course, and was glad that Kat was getting the same training he had.

Part of him felt guilty for doing what they were doing. He had originally kept these excursions secret from Kat, and he had been an idiot for doing so. But here he was again, about to do the same thing. Sure, he had his wife's permission now, but he knew she didn't like it. And he hated having to do something she didn't like. If he had any other choice...

"Well, that should about do it for now." Lance gave Kat's

suit one more check, then gave it a solid pat. "This looks to be working just fine. Now then, it's getting about that time."

Sergio nodded and looked at Kat. They couldn't hug goodbye while stuck in their exosuits. But he gave her a slight nod, which she returned. Whatever happened tonight, they were on the same page. And Sergio could appreciate that.

It seemed to take longer than usual to reach the foothills. Sergio felt the weight of the suit on his body as they walked up the now-familiar road. They cleared the mile or so it took to get there, rising the entire time until they crested the first foothill and stood at the little clearing there.

"Well then, here we are." Lance looked at his wrist watch. "If all goes the same as before, they should arrive in about seven minutes."

The keyword was 'if' all goes the same. With everything that had happened over the last two months, with the full exposure of Norma's ghost, neither of them knew if it would all work out the same this time. Norma seemed to be in charge, and that was enough to worry Sergio. With someone in charge, it was no longer a story of man against nature. It was a story of man against...well against something just as intelligent as man.

Sergio heard the first screams just on time. Well, at least one thing remained familiar. The ghosts were here. He readied himself.

The first ghost appeared not far ahead of him, drifting in their direction. Sergio let the flamethrowers out, drawing the ghost in like before with the lure of the fire's energy. His heart began to pound as the apparition drew closer. Just...a little...more.

He jabbed the iron spike into the ghost. It screamed, far

more loudly than ever before, and Sergio could see that the blood solution that Lance had concocted seemed to be working. The spike impaled the ghost in its midsection, as if it were corporeal.

A surge of triumph ran through Sergio. It was working! A moment later, the ghost disappeared, carried through the iron spike and conducted into the electrical loop that Lance had devised. Sergio felt the metal on his back grow warm, despite the insulation surrounding the iron. The ghost's scream escalated, much as a microphone experiencing a feedback loop. It rose until suddenly it popped out of existence. From what Sergio could tell, the ghost was gone. For good.

He turned to the next ghost, much more confident this time. Lance stood at his side, having watched the full experience. "Whoop! It works! We've got this, Sergio."

Sergio grinned. That old feeling of elation returned. He was born for this!

The next ghost swooped in on him, and he quickly dispatched it like the first. A third came, then a fourth. None succeeded. A quick glance told him that Lance was having similar success. It was just like before, but this time, it looked like they were cleaning up the apparitions for good.

One by one the ghosts began to disappear. The clearing became more and more empty, until there were hardly any ghosts left. Sergio and Lance closed in on the last ones, a glint of triumph in their eyes. Finally, they had the upper hand.

A few moments later, and they were the only figures in the clearing. Not a single ghost remained.

Sergio banged his arms together with a loud clang as metal met metal. "I think we did it."

Silence greeted them both, blessed silence. "I think you're right, son. No sign of Norma though."

Sergio had realized the same thing. They had taken out the ghosts, but they hadn't seen any sign of the red-eyed leader. "Perhaps she is still recovering somehow? Or maybe she just knew she couldn't fight us like this."

"I hope it's something like that."

Sergio heard something. It started like a low rumble in the distance, but soon escalated until he could make it out clearly. It was a laugh, a terrifying female laugh. It rose until it filled the entire clearing. There was no mistaking it. That was Norma's laugh, but much more gleeful and powerful than Sergio had ever heard.

Something was very, very wrong.

"YOU FOOLS!" the voice boomed across the clearing. It was far louder than they'd heard before. Sergio and Lance reacted by standing back to back. Neither could see the ghost yet. "YOU THINK YOU CAN DEFEAT ME? I AM NOT TIED TO YOUR MORTAL REALM IN SUCH A WAY. I CANNOT DIE LIKE YOU. I AM NOTHING LIKE YOU."

Finally, the ghostly visage of Norma appeared before them. Larger than ever before, her red eyes bathing the clearing with their light.

Sergio couldn't think of anything to say. He had a sinking feeling that they had missed something. That Norma knew far more about the situation than they had supposed. Had she played them all?

"We took out your little minions," said Lance. "We hurt you before, we can hurt you again." He brandished his spikes in her direction.

Sergio thought he saw the apparition drift away from the spikes, ever so slightly. Keeping them out of reach. Good, so maybe the ghost wasn't invincible to their attacks yet. But that didn't stop Sergio's stomach from turning. They were definitely missing something.

"YOU TOOK AWAY SOME OF THE DEAD, THAT'S TRUE." Norma cackled. "BUT DO YOU HAVE ANY IDEA HOW MANY PEOPLE HAVE DIED, EVEN IN THIS TOWN ALONE, SINCE MAN FIRST SET FOOT UPON THIS WORLD. AND YOU THINK YOU'VE WON BY ELIMINATING A FEW DOZEN."

Sergio swallowed. There it was, that's what they were missing. They weren't just dealing with a few small-fry ghosts. This was something a lot bigger.

"I AM A GODDESS OF DEATH HERE. I HOLD POWER OVER THE DEAD, MORE POWER NOW THAN EVER BEFORE. AND I SUMMON THEM!"

Screams echoed across the clearing. Sergio turned. More apparitions were appearing from all sides.

Hundreds of them.

He remembered his promise to Kat. Grabbing Lance by the arm, he said, "Lance, we need to get out of here."

"We can't let them into the city." Lance was frightened, but determined. He held his stance, readying himself for the onslaught of ghostly images.

"Lance," he turned the detective to face him. "We will die if we stay. These ghosts are entering the city whether we want them to or not. We can do nothing if we're dead."

Lucidity touched Lance's eyes, and he nodded. "Very well."

They ran.

Ghosts came at them, while Norma's ghost cackled with glee. "RUN! RUN! I HAVE ALREADY WON. I HAVE MORE POWER NOW THAN I HAVE EVER FELT BEFORE. I HAVE A FOUNDER!"

Sergio froze in his tracks. He turned to face the apparition, only absently spearing a few lesser ghosts that halted next to him. But for a moment, the clearing stood still. No more ghosts attacked him.

"What do you mean?" he said, staring up at Norma's huge form.

"EXACTLY WHAT I SAID. AND EXACTLY WHAT YOU FEAR."

"You...you didn't." Cold dread settled into Sergio's heart.

"SHE'S WITH ME NOW." This last pronouncement heralded a new laugh. It followed Sergio as he spun and ran for all he was worth, back to his home. Other ghostly voices joined in the laugh, and soon it seemed like the entire mountainside was laughing at his back as he ran.

He could hear Lance trailing behind him, hear him shouting for Sergio to slow down. But Sergio would not. Disregarding all else, he stripped his exosuit from his arms and back. They were only slowing him down. Redoubling his efforts, he sprinted down the foothill.

No ghosts followed. They remained in place. Sergio could hear their laughter fading as he put more and more distance between them.

He arrived at the door to his house in record time. He tried to open the door, but it was locked. Fumbling with his keys, he cursed as he dropped them.

A few terribly long moments later, he recovered the keys and unlocked the door. He saw nothing, heard nothing.

"Kat!" he shouted. No response.

He threw open the door to the master bedroom. His eyes found his wife, and he almost collapsed to the floor.

Kat was lying on the floor, her exosuit broken and mangled around her. Her flesh was pale, as cold as ice. Her lips were a dark blue, but Sergio nearly gasped with relief as he saw them move. She was still alive.

Feeling a surge of strength, he lifted Kat into his arms and held her, feeling his own body chill as her skin made contact with his. She was in an advanced stage of hypothermia, but she was still alive. At least there was that much. He thought he felt her shudder. She was trying to say something.

"A-al.."

Alice! Setting Kat down gently under the covers, he rushed into the other room. Alice was nowhere to be seen. He checked her playpen, under the furniture, in the bathroom, and their spare room. Alice was gone.

It was only when he returned to the bedroom that he first noticed Simon was still there. He must have been under the bed or something when Sergio first arrived. Now he was curled atop the bed, next to Kat but above the sheets. He was sitting in the fetal position, his arms hugging his knees, and he was rocking back and forth.

Lance came bolting through the door, having finally caught up to Sergio. He entered just as Simon opened his mouth to speak.

"Bad things happen."

CHAPTER 10

"I'LL ADMIT, THIS IS HARD FOR ME TO READ. I WASN'T THERE
FOR THIS PART, AND SEEING MOM IN SUCH PAIN IS
AGONIZING. IT WASN'T THE FIRST TIME I SAW MOM
LIKE THIS."

Kat was still alive. It had been hard. That first night, no one really knew if she would survive, Kat included. She had never been so cold in her life. But, after drinking some warm liquids, and being held in bed all night by Sergio, she finally started to feel better.

Even so, some of her nerve ends had been damaged and she spent several days feeling like parts of her were numb. Luckily no lasting damage had been done, and after a few weeks, she was back to normal.

Well, normal was a relative term. Sure, she was back to physical health, but she was not okay. Not at all.

Her Alice was gone, and had been since that night. For all Kat knew, she was dead. They had searched everywhere they could think of. Norma's house, the granary, the police station, even the foothills. They found nothing. No trace. Kat had seen the ghosts take her little girl away from her, while she lay on the ground too weak to intervene.

Add to that the fact that searching the town was extremely dangerous now. After failing to stop Norma during the previous month, the ghosts had roamed free, tearing through the town as they went, killing most. And, given the nature of the pocket universe they lived in, the inhabitants would eventually pop back into existence, only to be fed on again by the spirits.

Their only advantage now seemed to be that Norma had forgotten about them. To the ghosts that patrolled the streets, they were no more than any other living being in the town. That meant that they were not specifically targeted like Kat had been the night they took Alice. They wouldn't be able to withstand an attack from all the ghosts. But they could take care of the occasional passerby. Lance installed an iron barrier around their home which acted as a sort of guard against the ghosts, though not as efficient as a Faraday cage, which was what Sergio really wished they had. He claimed it would likely hide them from the ghosts completely.

Regardless, they continued to make regular excursions, wearing their exosuits and taking out the occasional ghost as they went. One always stayed behind to guard Simon, who they were sure still had something to do with all of this, though Norma had seemingly forgotten about him too.

Kat left the house at every chance she got. She had to find Alice. She had to! Nothing else mattered now. They had started a sweep of the entire town, going from house to house, from business to business, breaking in and searching every corner. They were long past caring about breaking and entering. The town was so overrun that most residents were dead, and the ones that weren't had died enough times that they were essentially mindless drones, fully under the influence of Norma and her minions.

That was what they were doing today. She and Lance were out, checking a street a few blocks over from their house. These patrols were about the only thing that kept

Kat sane. She could lose herself in the work, searching for her baby girl.

Approaching a house, she tested the door handle. It was locked. Without pausing, she stepped back and kicked the door for all she was worth. The hinge splintered, and with another kick, the door was open.

"Not very subtle." Lance followed Kat as they stepped through the threshold.

Inside they found a now familiar sight. A dead family in the living room, with a few stray ghosts drawing some residual energy from them. Kat pulsed her flamethrowers and the ghosts turned to see the source of the new energy. Their eyes glinted in the firelight, and Kat growled.

"Come and get it, filth." She brandished her iron spikes.

The ghosts did not disappoint. They hurdled towards her and Lance, eager for some new sources of energy to gorge on. But they never got their wish as Kat and Lance speared them with their iron spikes, causing them to cry out. In less than a minute, the ghosts that had occupied the house were gone, sucked into the feedback loop and destroyed. It was over too quick for Kat, who could feel her worry return as the adrenaline faded.

Perhaps this one, maybe she'll be here. That was what she told herself with each new building they entered, and it was the only thing that really kept Kat going.

But they searched the house from top to bottom and found nothing. Kat sighed and collapsed in the couch, next to one of the dead people.

"Lance, I can't do this anymore."

Lance turned to face her, blinking as he saw where she was sitting. "Don't say that, ma'am. You should be proud. Why all the ghosts you've killed since your recovery..."

"I don't want to kill ghosts, it does little good anyway. I just want to find Alice."

"Right, and that we will, ma'am. As long as one of us is alive, we'll find her eventually. It's only a matter of time."

Kat appreciated Lance's words, but they did little to comfort her now. "Let's go check the park again."

The park was one of those 'sources of power' that Lance went on about. They hadn't learned why, exactly, but Lance speculated that since Simon had gone there as a child, the place was likely a focal point for his mind, one that manifested itself in the ethereal magic of the town. Just more evidence that Simon was somehow the cause everything that was going on.

Kat and Lance arrived at the park without incident, though the moment they arrived, they knew they were in for a fight. Ghosts crowded the park, far more than real people had in the months prior. But it wasn't so many that the two of them couldn't handle it.

Kat stepped forward, brandishing her flamethrowers, feeling her adrenaline rise. She had grown to love that feeling; it was the only thing she felt anymore.

A ghost swooped in after her, and she speared it with her spike, reveling in its scream as it tried to escape her iron feedback loop. She turned to face the next one, and the next. Each one died in horrible screams, and Kat almost found herself smiling. It was not a smile of joy.

One by one, the spirits came to them, and one by one they disappeared in a scream. Lance stood his ground, but he was nowhere near as aggressive as Kat, who was a whirlwind of iron spikes and the screams of dying ghosts.

Soon, too soon, the ghosts were gone, and Kat collapsed on a bench, feeling her heart rate return to normal.

She was on the same bench that she used to sit on,

where she first met Simon and let Alice roam around her. Kat stared at the grass where she had watched Alice play. Her shoulders slumped, and tears came to her eyes. It was not the first time she'd cried for Alice, but it was the first time since those first few days after Alice's kidnapping. Since then, she'd managed to turn herself into steel. To focus on the search and on eliminating ghosts. But now, that was beginning to feel more and more useless.

She fell to her knees next to the bench and bent low, grabbing fistfuls of grass and pounding on the ground. Lance watched but said nothing, probably realizing that there was nothing he could do or say to comfort her.

Her cries turned to screams. She had never been so angry, not even when Anti-Sergio had captured her and killed that family. Even that horrible experience was nothing compared to this. At least she had known that Alice was safe with Sergio back then. Now, she had nothing.

She jerked back her head and let one final scream echo through the park. Then she collapsed back on the ground, breathing heavily. Lance only stood there.

Minutes later, she rose to her knees and wiped her eyes. "I'm..I'm sorry you had to see that."

"It's alright, ma'am. I understand. Truly, I do."

She pulled herself back onto the bench and Lance sat next to her. "You know," he continued. "I never did tell you everything about my past. I used to have a son, not much older than Simon. He's the one that slept in my spare bedroom, the one you two slept in that first night when you arrived."

Kat wiped her eyes, listening to Lance, intrigued.

"His mother and I met during the Depression. I was out of work, and looking for a job. I almost starved to death. She saved me."

"She gave you a job?"

"One day she just showed up, and gave me something to eat. Invited me into her home. She seemed to know me, though I hadn't seen her before that day. Told me that she was a member of a group that helped people."

Something clicked in Kat's mind. "Argo Force! She was a member?"

Lance nodded and fingered the Argo Force ring on his finger. "This was hers. She became the love of my life. We married, and spent a few years together. Then she got pregnant with my boy. Named him Leo, after my father. But she..." He choked. Kat put a hand on his shoulder. He patted it gratefully and continued. "She died giving birth. And a few years later, he died too. Pneumonia. They were all I had."

"Oh Lance. I'm sorry, I had no idea."

"It's alright, ma'am. I've found other hobbies to occupy me. Honestly, I think this whole ghost fiasco may have saved my life. It gave me purpose. And then having you and Sergio arrive. Well, it felt like having family again."

Kat gave him a hug, then settled into the bench, staring around at the trees around her. A question occurred to her. "Is she the one who trained you? Who taught you all these things about ghosts and pocket universes?"

Lance nodded. "She knew a lot, that one." He leaned back on the bench. "She used to tell me stories every night, like a little kid in storytime. Never once did I think I would one day need all of it. I just liked to hear her talk."

Kat looked away and stared ahead of her, imagining Alice playing in the grass ahead. Looked like she wasn't the only one who had been scarred in their association with Argo Force. She knew the organization had all the best intentions, but could it truly be worth everything that she, Lance, and probably countless others would go through?

Lance saw her staring at nothing and patted her on the shoulder. "Alice is still alive, Kat. You have to believe me on that. Norma has no use for her dead."

"Unless it was to somehow get her out of the way. Invergence wanted her dead, I think. I'm sure others would. Why not this ghost?"

"Because this ghost consumes energy. Alice is a Founder, or will be at least. Her destiny..."

"I know, I know. It creates a lot of cosmic energy or something. Don't fault a mother for being concerned anyway."

Lance pursed his lips. "It'll be okay, Kat. You'll see. Everything works out in the end."

Kat wanted to ask him how he could say something like that when his own wife and son had died. But before the words could form, she felt a familiar chill.

"HOW TOUCHING." Norma's voice echoed behind her. She spun and faced the ghost, mere feet away, a smile on her ethereal lips.

"What do you want?" she growled.

"WELL I SUPPOSE YOUR LAPDOG ALREADY TOLD YOU HOW I THRIVE ON ENERGY. PREFERABLY COSMIC ENERGY, THOUGH I ENJOY THE PHYSICAL STUFF WHEN IT COMES AROUND. BUT DO YOU KNOW WHAT CREATES ONE OF THE MOST POTENT FORMS OF COSMIC ENERGY?"

"I'm sure you're going to tell me."

Norma's pale face split into a grin. "PAIN. EMOTIONAL PAIN. AND RIGHT NOW, DEARIE, YOU'VE CREATED A RELATIVE FEAST!"

Kat let the anger boil within. "Where have you taken her?"

"OH, THE GIRL? OH, SHE'S SAFE, NEVER FEAR. I'VE TUCKED HER AWAY WHERE YOU WILL NEVER FIND HER."

"Give her back to me or I'll—"

"YOU'LL DO WHAT? YOUR ANGER IS ALREADY MAKING ME STRONGER. NOT NEARLY THE STRENGTH THAT YOUR LITTLE GIRL PROVIDES, BUT NOT BAD IF I DO SAY SO MYSELF."

Lance reached over to grab Kat's arm. "Come on, we should go."

But Kat had had enough. She swiped at the demon with her iron spikes, but all Norma did was float out of reach and laugh.

"AHAHAHA, DEARIE. PLEASE, YOU SHOULD KNOW BY NOW THAT YOU CAN'T HURT ME."

"So why don't you come closer and test that theory?"

Norma pursed her lips, if such a thing were possible for a ghost. "YOU KNOW, I JUST MIGHT KILL YOU. YOU'VE PROVIDED ME WITH SO MUCH, IT'S TRUE. BUT I'D CONSIDER IT A SACRIFICE WORTH MAKING IF IT MEANT YOU WERE OUT OF MY WAY."

"So I am a threat to you."

"OH, DON'T KID YOURSELF, CHILD. YOU ARE MERELY A NUISANCE TO ME. I HAVE ALL I WANT. SOON I WILL BREAK FREE OF THIS PLACE AND THAT WILL BE THE END OF THE LIFE YOU KNOW."

Lance tugged at Kat's arm again, and this time she followed. They set off down the road, heading towards the house. But in a flash of light, Norma disappeared and reappeared ahead of them, still high enough that Kat couldn't reach her with her spikes. "YOU'RE LEAVING?" she said in mock offense. "DID I MAKE YOU ANGRY? AHAHAHA, GOOD! ALL THE MORE FOR ME."

Kat realized what Norma was doing. She was trying to make Kat angry, to feed her with her suffering. Well, Kat would have none of that. Taking a few deep breaths, she did her best to quiet her mind and put one step in front of the other. Together, she and Lance kept advancing.

It was all Kat could do to keep from shouting, because Norma followed them, not disappearing like she had before. This time she was determined to haunt them until they went mad. Or at least, that's what it felt like to Kat. And it was beginning to work, too.

Soon they reached her front step, Norma still cackling and shrieking behind them.

"WHAT'S THIS? YOU'VE SET UP A WARD AGAINST ME?" Norma observed the iron bars surrounding the house. "HAVEN'T YOU LEARNED BY NOW THAT SUCH TOYS CAN'T HOLD ME?" And with that, she floated past them, through the front door.

Kat gasped. Sergio and Simon were in there! Without another word she bolted through the door. Simon was sitting next to Sergio on the couch, and both looked up at Norma with terrified eyes.

"Get away from them!" Kat screamed. Alice was gone, she was not going to let Norma take anyone else.

"OH, CALM YOURSELF, DEARIE. REMEMBER, I'M HERE TO FEED OFF YOU, AND I CAN'T DO THAT IF YOU'RE DEAD."

"What?" Sergio called out.

Kat knelt next to the couch, taking Simon in her arms. The poor boy looked frightened out of his wits. "She's not here for you, Simon. And she's not here to kill me, or she would have done it by now. Everything is going to be okay."

Norma cackled something else, but Kat did her best to tune it out. It was like dealing with an Internet troll, where responding only gave the person what they wanted. In Norma's case, that could be taken literally, if Kat's suffering produced some form of energy that the ghost could feed on. Perhaps that was why she had kept Simon in the basement before, to feed on his suffering. Just the thought made her wrap her arms tighter around the boy.

"Everything will be alright, child. I love you, my husband loves you. Lance loves you. We're here to take care of you. Okay?" She looked into the boy's face. There were tears in his eyes, but he was looking up at her, trusting her. She kept his gaze. "Focus on my face, Simon. See? I'm not afraid. My face is not afraid."

Simon reached out a hand and touched her face. Hope brushed his eyes, as if he had never before thought that one didn't have to be afraid. "Momma..." he turned to glance at Norma, who had gone silent for once and was staring at the boy.

Kat gently grabbed his face and brought it down until he was looking at her again. "I'm your Momma, Simon. I will keep you safe."

Simon hugged her, flinging both arms around her neck as tight as he could. Kat hugged him back.

"ARRGGGGG!" Norma screamed. It was a scream far worse than any Kat had heard before, even worse than when Lance had driven the spike into her ghostly form.

"WHAT HAVE YOU DONE! YOU, ALL OF YOU, THE BOY..." The woman, if she could be called that, was frantic. Staring from one to another. Then she doubled over and screamed again. Was she in pain?

"YOU!" She pointed at Kat. "THIS IS ALL YOUR DOING. WELL THAT SETTLES IT. I WILL SEE ALL OF

YOU DIE TONIGHT. YOU WILL BE A THORN IN MY SIDE NO LONGER."

And with that, she disappeared, simply faded away. But her leaving did not bring silence. Thousands of ghostly screams could be heard from all around the house. They were surrounded.

"Well," Lance swallowed. "Might I suggest the two of you suit up."

Kat didn't argue. She hastily lifted the metal harness and strapped it into place. Sergio ran to do the same with their third exosuit which was lying in the kitchen.

The screams were getting louder, still coming from all directions. But they had prepared for something like this. They knew it would come sooner or later.

Lance brought in the bottles. They were full of alcohol and contained a single drop of Simon's blood. A cloth had been shoved into the top. Kat grabbed one of the bottles and lit the cloth, getting ready to set off their first true defense.

Opening the window, she about dropped the flaming bottle. It was dusk, but she could clearly see the forms of the ghosts approaching their house. There had to be hundreds of them, thousands. More than Kat could count.

They were going to die tonight.

Kat pushed the thought away and flung the bottle out a few feet from their house. It hit the target square on. A roar echoed from outside as a line of oil ignited, circling their house in a matter of seconds. Now they just had to hope that it didn't come close enough or burn hot enough to set the house on fire.

The oil had also contained trace amounts of Simon's blood, which explained why the ghosts hesitated as they drew closer.

But as before, the ghosts were attracted to the flames.

They could not keep themselves from diving at the fiery moat. Shrieks echoed from all around the house as dozens of the apparitions met a fiery end in the blood.

But there were far more than a few dozen ghosts. Slowly, but steadily, the fire began to die. In the dimming light, many ghosts forgot about the flames and floated up and beyond, straight towards the window where Kat stood waiting.

She dug her iron spikes, coated in the blood-resin solution that Lance had concocted, into the first ghost. It screamed, was caught by the conductive iron feedback loop, and winked out of existence with a satisfying pop.

But Kat had no time to take any satisfaction in the ghost's extermination. For more ghosts were rapidly approaching. She took out a few more at the window, but these ghosts didn't need an open space to attack. They floated through the wall, flanking her from the side. So she backed away and continued to take them out one by one.

A quick glance told her that Sergio and Lance were doing the same. Sergio covered the back wall, while Lance was doing his best to take out ghosts on the sides. Simon stood between the three, looking strangely calm, as if Kat's comfort earlier had truly convinced him that he would be safe. Kat grimaced. Perhaps she had been too hasty to make this kind of promises.

She turned back to her work and barely managed to save herself from a ghost who swooped in from the ceiling. Adrenaline pumping, she called out, "Lance! Why isn't the iron perimeter working?"

"It is," Sergio shouted an answer instead, while still fending off a pair of ghosts. "I saw some of them run right into it, but there are just too many, the iron can't suck them all in."

And Kat supposed that the iron only protected them from ghosts coming at a specific angle. If they came through the roof...

As if reading her thoughts, another ghost entered through the ceiling, and then another. Kat took them both down, but then a piercing cold entered her right leg. She felt herself fall to one knee. Looking down, she saw a ghost had come from the ground below, and now held onto her right leg. Kat could almost see her leg turning blue as she lost all feeling on that side.

She stabbed at the ghost and it disappeared in a flurry of screams. But the damage was done. She could no longer stand, and she wouldn't last long on the ground like this.

"Kat!" Sergio was at her side, keeping away the ghosts that had swooped in for the kill. Lance too stepped closer to Kat, standing back to back with Sergio. Simon only stepped beside Kat, looking...confused.

"I'm sorry, Simon."

"Momma..."

"Everything will be fine," she lied. "We'll get through this." But Simon could see the tears in Kat's eyes. A resolute expression crossed his face, and he hugged Kat. Ghosts were closing in, but Kat hugged him back, ignoring the threats. She felt her arms grow cold next, and the loss of feeling caused her to fall on her back.

As her eyes dimmed, she saw Lance and Sergio each fall to the ground as their own legs froze and collapsed. They kept fighting, but more and more ghosts were closing in. Kat's vision was full of them. Her last conscious thought was to recognize that Simon was still hugging her. And then the cold extended to her head, and she knew no more.

CHAPTER 11

"NOW THIS PART I DEFINITELY REMEMBER. BUT FOR SOME WEIRD REASON THIS IS A MEMORY THAT ACTUALLY GREW STRONGER AS I AGED."

K at drifted in the light. She had experienced this sensation before, floating, no, traveling through emptiness. She wanted to follow the light, to explore that great adventure to...

A cold vice took hold of her and jerked her away from the warm light. She gasped and suddenly everything was lucid. Her eyes stared wide all around her.

And for a moment, she wondered if she was going mad. She felt...strange. Like she was two people, or more than two people at once. Part of her was familiar, part felt like she was a little child again, and another part felt like she was an old woman full of wisdom, experience, sorrow, and something else as well. Something dark.

She lay on the ground, or at least on something hard. When she looked at it, all she saw was a gray mist and no sign of earth, wood, or anything else that would constitute a ground. She glanced up to see that the air around her looked the same, full of a misty gray darkness. She could see nothing in any direction.

But she could hear something. Long moans coming

from human mouths, or at least they sounded human. And something else. Kat strained her ears to listen. It almost sounded like a...river.

"Kat!" A voice called out. Kat nearly jumped for joy. It was Sergio's voice.

"Sergio, yes, I'm here!"

"Kat, where are you?" His voice was closer now.

They continued to call out to each other until Kat could finally make out his form, stumbling through the mist just ahead of her. He saw her too, and they rushed into each other's arms. For a moment, they just stood there, saying nothing, only enjoying the embrace.

Kat leaned up and kissed him. "I thought you were dead."

"I thought we all were dead. Although," he glanced around nervously. "I'm not entirely certain that we're alive either."

It wasn't a thought Kat enjoyed, but she had no explanation for where they were or why. The last thing she remembered was being attacked by ghosts from all sides, her arms and body going limp. She should have died, and perhaps she did.

"Where's Lance?" she asked.

"Oi!" a voice cried out as if to answer her question. "Get your hands off me!"

Kat looked at Sergio who shared the same concerned look on his face. Lance was in trouble. They sprinted in the direction of the noise, and soon saw two figures in the gray darkness. One was unmistakably Lance, but the other was a pale shadow. A ghost!

Kat and Sergio ran to place themselves between the ghost and Lance, though all three of them had somehow lost their exosuits, therefore Kat had no idea how they were going to fight this ghost. It...

It wasn't making any aggressive movement, simply standing there with hands outreached, pointing.

"Well, hi there, Sergio, ma'am." Lance didn't sound like he was in distress. "I thought I was alone here, save for this creep." He pointed at the ghost. "Not behaving like I would expect. He keeps pointing me in that there direction, and when I tried to go the other way, he pushed me. His form didn't pass through me or nothin'."

Now that Kat could see the ghost a little better, she noticed that he didn't look exactly like the other ghosts. His face was more human-like, and his form, though still translucent, had a solidarity to it that she hadn't seen before. And it didn't have that sickly glow that the other ghosts carried.

"Uh..." she spoke to the ghost. "Hello, do you want us to go somewhere?"

The ghost nodded.

"Where, may I ask?"

The ghost held up an arm, pointing.

Kat kept an eye on the ghost, then started walking in the opposite direction it indicated. The ghost moved to intercept, shaking its head and holding one hand out to stop her. She turned to look at Sergio and Lance. Sergio shrugged, "We've nowhere else to go at the moment."

Kat agreed with that, though she didn't like the idea of following a ghost. Regardless, she turned to the apparition, "Lead the way. We'll follow."

The ghost nodded and drifted past her. With a deep breath, Kat followed, with Lance and Sergio trailing behind her.

They walked for what seemed like hours, but might have

been minutes. Time almost didn't seem to work the same here. Every time Kat inquired about where they were going, or how much time it would take, their guide remained silent.

But soon they had other things to think about. Other ghostly figures were now walking with them, taking no notice of their party, but drifting in the same direction. Kat also realized that the sound of a river was growing louder. It seemed like the closer they approached the sound, the more ghosts she could see. But these ghosts were not hostile, not as before. They simply moved forward, as if drawn to something.

At last, they could see the river ahead of them. As they approached, they drew alongside and their guide pointed ahead in the direction the river flowed. Apparently they needed to follow the water.

But Kat grew uncomfortable as she observed the river more closely. It was filthy, full of dirt and oil and slime. She couldn't even understand how it was flowing so fast. It looked like sewage. No, worse than sewage. And it stank.

Suddenly, Sergio stopped and caught hold of Kat's arm. "Do you see that?"

Kat peered through the grayness. She could see something. Two forms, facing each other in the distance. One was tall and looked less solid than the other. The second...

"Simon!" she bounded forward. The figure turned to face her. It was indeed Simon, though he looked different, older. He smiled as she approached. The other figure he had been talking to, hurried away leaving Simon alone.

"Hello, Kat," he said. His voice was far more mature than one would expect from a six-year-old. As Kat looked at him up close, she saw that he seemed to...shimmer. That was the only word Kat could think of. In one moment, she was looking at the young boy she knew, and in others she thought she could see a grown man in front of her. It was a disconcerting experience.

"What...?" was all she could get out as she looked at him, confused.

"Hold on there, son," Lance said. "Something's not right with you."

Simon smiled. "You're seeing my future form. This place, it's not like Earth. Here, you are young, and old at the same time. There's no linear experience of time."

"Ah!" Lance grew excited. "So that explains why I've been feeling smart and dumb at the same time."

That also explained what Kat had felt when she first arrived, though the feeling had settled now. Sergio, however, looked troubled. "So you're saying, that you are essentially the child we know and an adult as well? How does that work?"

"Time simply works differently here, it's more of an afterthought."

"And just exactly where is here?"

"This place has gone by many names. Purgatory, Spirit Prison, Hell, though Hell is actually something else. Those who are slightly more informed called it the Astral Plane. It's a sort of second layer on Earth, an in-between space.

"And why, exactly, are we here?"

"Because you died."

That sobered everyone up. "You're saying that the ghosts won? That we died trying to fight Norma."

"Sort of, but you're forgetting one thing."

"The pocket universe," Lance said, putting it together first.

"We'll come back to life," Sergio said.

"That's right." Simon nodded.

"But will we still be ourselves?" Kat felt worry creep in on her again. "The others, once they came back to life, they were different. More like zombies. Is that what will happen to us?"

Simon smiled again. "No, because you have something the others did not."

"What?"

"Me."

And he began to explain everything.

"I have an unusual connection to this place. As a young child, I suffered more than anyone had in Greenfield for many years. It was a brand new town, with little suffering tainting it. When I was abandoned and left to fend for myself, nearly dying in the park, I saw my mother come to me."

Kat nodded. They had learned this much in their research.

"My child's mind knew she was gone, but at the same time, I didn't doubt that she had returned. Now I know that my mother wasn't really my mother at all. She was a ghost, attracted to me by my suffering. At the time, she was no different than any other ghost that you've encountered. There was nothing special about her."

"So what happened?" Sergio asked. He sat enraptured with the explanation.

"In my acceptance of her as my mother, I forged a bond between us. One that when strengthened left me weaker, and made her stronger. She fed on me and my suffering." He turned to Kat. "Until you came."

"What did I have to do with it?"

"When I first met you and Alice, the bond between me and Norma strained. She imprisoned and tortured me to try and increase my suffering, to feed on me still. But there was nothing she could do. So she let me go when you came for me. She thought I was of no more use to her."

"She thought?" Kat leaned in closer.

"The bond still existed, it was just weakened by my interactions with you. What she didn't know until recently was that our bond could be cut off, and that doing so would cause her to lose all the strength she gained from me."

"And the other ghosts, the ones that follow Norma?" Lance asked.

"They would also disappear. That rift in the foothills was a byproduct of my forging a bond with Norma. It will close as soon as the bond is broken."

"So you're saying that we nearly broke that bond?"

Simon nodded. "We were close. But we are strangely fortunate that we didn't."

"Why?"

"Because she now has another source of power. Not a bond like mine, but enough to make her a force to be reckoned with."

"Alice." Kat breathed the word out.

"That's right. If we had closed the breach, she would have remained here, and we would have had no way to retrieve her."

"You're saying she's here, in this...Astral Plane?"

"And as long as Norma has her, she will remain a queen among the dead."

Kat felt like she should be doing something, not just standing here. "Well then, we have to go get her. Where is she?"

Simon smiled. "We follow the river."

Kat, Sergio, and Lance fell into line as Simon began leading them to wherever Norma held Alice. After a few minutes of walking Kat drew closer to Simon.

"Who were you talking to when we arrived?"

"That was my father." Simon kept staring at the ground in front of them.

"The one who died in the war?"

"Mhmm. I thought meeting him in this place might help me come to terms with his death. It may have. I'm not sure. We'll see how my young self reacts when we return to the real world."

Kat had a million more questions for him, like how did that one ghost lead them to Simon, or what was the river. But she kept these to herself for now. Simon, though seemingly wiser and more capable than the child she had known, still had a look of sorrow on his face. She wouldn't bother him further.

Suddenly, Simon halted. Kat and the others stopped too, though Lance nearly collided with Sergio before doing so.

"We are close." Simon was listening for something Kat could not hear. "Norma has guards ahead. I have less control over these but perhaps..."

A familiar scream sounded ahead of them, and Kat steeled herself. How were they supposed to fight these demons without suits or anything else to aid them.

A half-dozen figures came floating at them in the darkness. Like the other ghosts they'd seen, they seemed more solid here, but no less frightening. Simon's face was bunched up in concentration. Then in a moment, he raised a hand and yelled.

The ghosts vanished into nothingness, as quick as they had come. Simon gasped as if he had been holding his breath for a long time. "That...I wasn't sure I could do that."

"What exactly did you do?" Kat was still staring at the spot where the ghosts had disappeared.

"I...think I killed them, or the ghost equivalent. I sent them to the Place Beyond."

Kat didn't ask what that was, for in that moment, she began to see something else ahead of them. Something called to her, and she pushed ahead of Simon to discover what it was.

She saw a lone bed, simple with no furnishings, lying in the middle of nowhere. It had on clean, white sheets, and on the bed sat a child.

Kat swallowed. Sergio walked to her side. He too was staring at the bed.

"I...is it?" he asked.

Kat rushed forward and rounded the bed in a matter of seconds. There, she saw the face of the child. That precious face that she recognized instantly.

"Alice," she choked and felt tears sting her eyes. "Alice!"

She fell on the little girl, hugging her to her chest as tight as she dared. Like Simon, the girl shimmered as she seemed to pass from age to age, sometimes looking like the child Kat knew, and sometimes older, more experienced. But her expression remained weary, troubled, and dazed.

"Mother?" she said. "Is it you?"

"Yes, it's me, love." Kat didn't even bother to remark on how mature her daughter sounded.

"I hurt all over," Alice said. "She's kept me here for so long."

"We're going to get you out, Alice. We're here to help." This time it was Sergio providing the comforting words. Kat had her hand to her mouth, barely able to hold herself together.

"I wish none of this had happened to you. I'm so sorry."

"You don't need to be sorry. In this place, I...I can feel

what I will become. You and father. You are more important than you realize."

"But why do we have to go through all this heartache. I couldn't bear the thought of losing you. It was almost too much." Kat was sobbing audibly now, the tears streaming down her cheeks as she cupped Alice's face in her hands.

Alice smiled for the first time. "The hotter the fire, the stronger the forge. All of this, everything you've experienced, it's shaping you, and shaping me through you. In time, you will become Legends whispered about throughout the universe. For you raised a Founder."

"I don't want you to have a hard life."

"Nothing great was ever achieved without hardship."

Kat felt herself grow determined. "Let's get you out of here." She stood and began to lift her daughter. She felt a strange sensation of trying to lift a child, but also a heavier adult. She almost stumbled as she felt the girl's weight. Sergio instantly stepped forward to help.

But Alice resisted, the weariness back in her face. "She won't let me leave."

"I believe I can help with that." Simon drew closer to Alice. "I have a little strength I can share. Let me help you."

He took Alice by one arm and gently lifted, helping Alice rise to her feet. She met his eyes, and Kat thought she saw an understanding pass between them. Then they all turned and began walking in the direction they had come, following Simon who seemed to be the only one who knew where he was going in the shadows.

"We have to hurry to the rift, it's not far." Simon quickened his step. "She'll realize that Alice is gone soon."

As if hearing Simon's pronouncement, the world around them shuddered. What sounded like thunder cracked the fog and a terrible voice boomed through the darkness.

"WHERE HAS SHE GONE? FIND HER!"

"Run," said Simon.

They did their best. Alice still couldn't move very fast, but with support from her parents, they managed to move much faster than before.

Ghosts appeared in their vision, but Simon, running ahead of them, raised his hands and disintegrated the onslaught. Ghosts vanished as soon as they appeared, but the damage had already been done. Wails from the dying demons alerted Norma to their location.

Darkness grew, obscuring everything in their view. Simon stopped in his tracks, and the rest of them nearly collided with the boy. "She's here."

Two enormous red eyes appeared above them, as large as the sun, as bright as the moon. They could barely make out a face surrounding the eyes, seemingly made of the mists themselves. It's like the being was the mist, and had been the entire time.

Cold tendrils of darkness grabbed each of them. They cried out, and Alice let out a small whimper. "YOU COME INTO MY DOMAIN, TAKE SOMETHING THAT IS MINE, AND EXPECT TO GET AWAY WITH IT!"

Despite everything, despite the fear surrounding Kat's heart, she knew nothing but defiance in that moment. "She was never yours!"

Norma...or whatever Norma had become, paused, as if almost taken aback by Kat's defiance in the face of overwhelming power. "HOW ARE YOU CONSCIOUS HERE? YOU SHOULD HAVE LEFT THIS PLACE BY NOW, SIPHONED OFF TO THE PLACE BEYOND OR BACK TO YOUR BODY IN GREENFIELD UNDER MY CONTROL. AH, BUT OF COURSE. MY LITTLE PROTEGE

PROTECTED YOU. NO MATTER, THE PLACE BEYOND IS FAR TOO GOOD FOR YOU!"

Suddenly, Kat felt indescribable pain. She threw back her head and screamed as waves of torment shot through the dark tendrils that held her and into her body. If she had been in the physical realm, the pain would have been enough to kill her or knock her unconscious. In this plane, however, she felt every moment of it.

She couldn't see, couldn't think, couldn't hear if the others were trying to save her, or if they too were wrapped up in the same torment.

And then, in a heartbeat, she felt the power release her. She was acutely aware of how different she felt without a physical body. She instinctively wanted to take deep breaths, but her lungs didn't need air. She felt no residual pain, no adrenaline. She had simply been in pain, and now it was gone.

Looking up, she noticed that the rest of their company had also been released by the dark tendrils. Like Kat, they had fallen to the floor and looked like she felt.

Only Simon stood tall and still, facing the dark power that had once called itself his mother. The red eyes shifted to regard the boy, a pinprick of light standing up to an ocean of shadow.

"AH. OF COURSE. IN THIS PLACE YOU WOULD HAVE SOME POWER. BUT THAT WILL NOT BE ENOUGH TO HURT ME, BOY."

"I don't need to hurt you." Simon raised his hands above his head. "I just need to hold you."

What looked like a shield of light burst from Simon's fingertips. It radiated out in all directions, filling the space between them and Norma. A dark tendril prodded the makeshift shield, and recoiled as it disintegrated at the touch.

"GO!" Simon yelled. "You can see the breach from here!"

They turned to look, and sure enough, a thin white line extended a few hundred yards away, waving to and fro and emitting short bursts of light. Kat had no idea what a portal to another realm was supposed to look like, but if that wasn't a tear in the fabric of time and space, she didn't know what else was.

"LET ME GO, YOU WELP!" The darkness threw itself at the barrier Simon had created. Simon winced and the barrier hiccuped for a moment, before stabilizing once again.

"Let's go!" Lance was taking the lead, grabbing Alice in his arms and running as fast as he could. Sergio followed. But Kat hesitated, looking back at Simon. "We can't leave you!"

"Everything will be alright!" He yelled back. His words echoed what Kat had said to him, as a young boy, on several occasions.

"How can you know that? If we leave you with her..."

"I told you, in this place there is little concept of time. I know everything will be alright, that you will save me, just as I know that one day when I am older, I will be the one to save a pair of weary and injured travelers, carrying their newborn child."

He met her eyes then, and Kat saw it for just a moment. She saw the wisdom of an old man, the man Simon would become. She knew those eyes.

"Kat, we have to leave!" Sergio had returned for her, and was tugging on her arm. "Katariina, let's go."

She stared at Simon a moment longer, who gave her the briefest of nods.

"And Alice," said Simon, calling back to the girl who stood supported by Sergio and Lance. Alice turned to look at Simon.

"Find me!" he said, meeting her eyes. His barrier strained and Norma pushed in for the final push. Kat ran, catching up with Lance and family.

"It was Simon," she said aloud as she joined Sergio. "Our Simon."

Sergio didn't appear to hear her, but she knew. Of all the Simons in the world, they had taken in the one who would help them many years later as an old, grown man. They had only known that man for a matter of weeks, but they had been some of the most enjoyable in the time that Invergence had pursued them. He had saved them on more than one occasion, and now they were abandoning him to a monster.

They were going to save him. She didn't know how, but they were going to fix this, even if it killed her. That was the last thought she had, before hurling herself into the breach.

CHAPTER 12

"ONCE AGAIN, GUESS WHO SAVES THE DAY?!"

Kat awoke in her comfortable pajamas and stretched. Time to start the day! Sergio was already on his way out, so she kissed him goodbye and waved as he took off.

Alice was awake now, kicking and screaming, the cute little girl. Kat put her in the playpen and set about making herself and her child a little breakfast. The girl needed her nutrients to grow strong and beautiful after all.

When she was finished, she took some mashed up avocado and tried to feed it to the little girl. She resisted, a permanent look of distaste on her face. Kat coaxed and prodded, eventually managing to slip the food into Alice's mouth. Alice made a face and began to cry. "Oh well," Kat said, "We all have to do things that we don't like, don't we. It helps us grow into smart beautiful people. Yes it does, yes it does!" She put her face close to Alice's and nuzzled it with her nose.

But Alice remained upset for the rest of the morning. *Oh well, she'll get over it eventually,* Kat thought cheerily. Now was the time to clean up the house, and make it extra special for when Sergio returned home from work. He was so hard-working, and deserved the best that Kat could provide for him at home. Perhaps, if she finished in good time, she could take Alice to the park.

She set to work, first cleaning the bathroom, then the kitchen and the windows. Next, she began tidying up the living room. By that time, it was almost lunch, so she lit the stove and began to cook one of her favorite dishes, the...*wait a moment*. She didn't like to cook, did she? When had this started? She looked at all the ingredients she had laid out on the counter. What....what exactly had she been planning to do with all that?

But then a moment later she remembered and set to work mixing food in a bowl and preparing it to fry in her largest pan. She sung while she worked, if only to drown out the crying from her daughter. Honestly, she had just changed and fed her. What more could she want now?

Ignoring the cries for just a moment, Kat prepared a piece of dough to go in the frying pan. Fried scones, her favorite. Not exactly the best recipe to keep her tummy down, but worth it now and then. She placed the first lump of dough into the frying pan and watched as it browned.

Now, how long exactly was she supposed to leave it in there? What was the oil temperature supposed to be? For a moment, she lost a hold of the answers and watched as the scone began to brown further. She stood enraptured as the hot oil quickly burned the outside of the scone, leaving the inside relatively uncooked. The edges began to give off a light smoke as they burned. The smoke reminded Kat of something.

"Oh! Goodness me." She snapped out of her trance and took the scone out of the oil. "Oh, this will not do at all." She threw it away. "What on Earth was I frying it that hot for?"

She finished making lunch not long after and enjoyed the luscious hot bread with honey, savoring every bite. Upon finishing the meal, she felt very satisfied. Alice, on the other hand, was still upset, and had been all day. Perhaps now would be a good time to take a stroll outside. Yes, that sounded like a wonderful time!

She dressed Alice in something more suitable and placed her in the stroller. "Now, come along Alice. We don't want to be all fussy fuss in front of all the nice ladies in the park. What will they think?"

Smiling, she exited the house, pushing the stroller in front of her, and enjoying the nice weather as she walked. She loved pouring rain. It made everything seem so fresh. For some reason, the rain only made Alice even more upset. Didn't she realize how important water was to their little town?

They were both drenched from head to toe once they reached the park, and Kat was loving it. She found a bench to sit on, and let Alice out of her stroller. But the girl didn't seem to have much interest in crawling around. *Well, probably for the best,* Kat thought. This way, she didn't have to worry too much about what the baby girl was doing.

In the distance, she saw a nice little boy, a few years older than Alice. Maybe five or six. He had mousy brown hair and he stared at Kat and Alice from a distance. Kat waved, wondering why she thought she recognized the boy. She was sure she had never seen him before.

A woman walked up to the little one, took his hand and led him away. She was a nice-looking woman, with blonde hair and beautiful red eyes. Kat wished she could have red eyes like that one.

Alice let out a particularly loud wail and reached for Kat like she wanted to be held. Kat obliged and bounced the girl up and down, still feeling the cool refreshing feeling of the rain on her head. "What's the matter, girl. Are you scared of the nice people? I think you are. Maybe we should go say hi so you're not scared anymore."

She rose from the bench and began walking in the direction of the young boy and his mother. Perhaps then Alice would...

Kat felt a flash of pain in her head and she nearly dropped Alice as she doubled over, one hand to her head. She thought she saw images, memories that she didn't understand. A dark place, a scary monster with red eyes, a boy just like the one she saw ahead of her. Or perhaps it wasn't the same boy. The one she thought she saw was older, more mature. But it still looked like the same boy.

Alice stopped crying momentarily, but then Kat's headache faded and the girl took up her wailing again. The little one was beginning to get a chill from the rain. Yes, perhaps it was time to go back indoors again. Kat also wasn't feeling at all well. Perhaps a short nap would help her disposition. That sounded lovely.

She placed Alice back in her stroller and walked through the pouring rain towards her house. She waved to the neighbors that walked past, the solid ones and the transparent ones. They were all such nice people.

She thought she felt the headache returning, so she increased her step to get home.

But when she arrived, she saw someone waiting at the door. He was a man, in his late thirties perhaps, with a long trench coat and a hat on his head. He also looked familiar, though Kat had no idea where she had seen him before.

"Hello!" she said as she approached. The stranger paused as he considered her.

"I...I'm not sure why I'm here. I was just walking down this here street when I saw your house and...do I know you?"

"I'm certain you don't. But you look familiar."

"My name is Lance, I'm a detective. Live just a few blocks from here."

"So nice to meet you, Lance. Care to come in out of the rain?"

"Oh, I don't want to be a burden on you, ma'am."

Kat felt like she agreed, why had she invited him in? She didn't want a strange man in her house while her husband was away. But she could still feel it now, a queer trust of this man Lance. Besides, little Alice had quieted the moment she saw him.

"Nonsense, you're all dripping wet. Come in and I'll get a fire going. My husband will be home soon, and we can all get to know each other."

Unlocking the door, she stepped inside and did as she promised, though first changed Alice into some fresh clothes. By the time the fire began to roar, she heard the door handle turn. In stepped Sergio, his clothes soaked through, just like the rest of them.

"Hey honey!" She ran to kiss him on the cheek.

"Who's this?" he asked, eying Lance.

"Oh, he's just a neighbor that stopped by. I thought we could get to know each other. Maybe enjoy a nice casserole."

Sergio extended a hand to Lance. "Have we met?" His eyes were narrowed, as if trying to remember something.

Alice was crying again. Kat went to calm her, feeling that headache acting up again. Really, the girl should learn to behave.

"Can't say for sure." Lance returned Sergio's handshake. "I don't live far, so maybe we've seen each other."

"No, I swear there's something more to it." Sergio ran a hand through his hair. "Did we ever...work out together?"

They continued talking while Kat set about preparing dinner, multitasking as she also tried to hold Alice in one arm. That girl was just...not...letting...Kat...work.

Alice screamed. It was a sustained, deliberate scream, not just the wail of a small child. And for some reason that Kat could not fathom, it pierced her soul. The headache returned, more painful than ever and she stopped what she was doing to lean on the counter, setting Alice down as she did so.

But this time, she wasn't the only one buckling under the pain. Lance and Sergio were also holding their heads.

"Alice. Stop it, little girl. You're being a naughty, naughty girl. Stop!" Kat gasped, in too much pain to do more.

Like before, she thought she saw images of the past, but this time they returned with far more clarity than she had seen before. That boy again. His name was Simon. The transparent neighbors, they had attacked her and her husband. That man Lance, he had been their friend. Why had she not remembered all of this before?

Alice's scream died, but strangely enough, Alice looked far more pleased than she had before the scream. "Mommy!" she said and patted Kat on the face from her perch on the counter. "Wuv you!"

It was the first time Kat had heard Alice say those particular words. They melted her heart, and she embraced her child, unsure why she was crying.

"I do know you." Lance was looking back and forth at Kat and Sergio. "That girl, she's important, isn't she. Or will be."

"Your name is Lance," Sergio said, as if discovering something life changing. His eyes were wide and his arms extended partway in front of him. "We did train together, you've been teaching me martial arts!"

"Crumbs, but I think you're right, son."

Kat could remember it too. How on Earth had they not remembered this before?

"Didn't we go somewhere together, somewhere dangerous." Sergio held a hand to his head. "I honestly can't remember more than a day or two ago. I could swear I've been here for years, but I have no memory of how I got here."

"We were attacked," Kat said. "By our neighbors, the translucent ones."

"I don't think those are neighbors at all." Lance began pacing the room. "I have a feeling that I've been fighting them for a long time."

"CURSES," a huge voice cried out. "WILL YOU NEVER SUBMIT!"

They spun in all directions, trying to find the source of the voice. Kat recognized it, and she knew instinctively that she hated the owner of that voice.

Gray tendrils of smoke-like mist began forming around them, and two red eyes appeared in their midst. "I SUPPOSE IN LETTING YOU ESCAPE, THE BOY GAVE YOU SOME FORM OF PROTECTION. BUT THAT WILL STOP EVENTUALLY ONCE I KILL YOU AGAIN, AND THEN AGAIN."

Kat remembered everything, the fog lifted from her brain. "You attacked us! You took Alice!"

"AND I WILL TAKE HER AGAIN. YOU WILL NOT BE ABLE TO FOLLOW US THIS TIME."

"And what about Simon?" Sergio shouted at the red eyes. Apparently he had remembered too.

"YOU MEAN THIS EMPTY SHELL!" And with that,

Simon appeared before them, his eyes blank. Kat ran to him, feeling his arms and his face. He was solid, not a ghost, but he gave no indication that he could see any of them.

Norma, yes that had been her name, laughed. "YOU CANNOT DESTROY ME NOW, YOUR ONLY WEAPON IS NOW UNDER MY POSSESSION. THE BOY REMEMBERS NOTHING. HE IS EMPTY INSIDE. HIS BOND REMAINS, BUT NOW I REAP ALL THE BENEFITS."

Dark tendrils extended to all three of them, and Kat felt, for the second time, the worst pain imaginable. She threw back her head and screamed.

ALICE WALKED AROUND THE TABLE. She could move on only her legs now, which was really nice for getting places. Mommy had forgotten about her when the scary lady arrived, so she managed to let herself down from the counter, not an easy thing. She almost fell twice.

The scary lady was making those loud noises again. Her mommy and daddy were talking to it, and that nice man too. They were making loud noises at the scary lady, though the scary lady was really much louder. Alice put her hands to her ears. She didn't like so much noise. In fact, she didn't like any of this. Maybe she would go to the other room and wait until all the noises went away. Yes, that was a good idea. She could play with her soft toy that Mommy called a bunny.

But then, she saw her friend, the boy. He appeared out of thin air. That was cool! Alice wished she could do that. The boy was good at things. But something was wrong with the boy. He wasn't smiling. Alice liked it when he smiled.

She took a few curious steps towards him. What did her

Mommy call him? Simey? That sounded right. Why wasn't Simey moving or doing anything. He almost always came to play with her.

She took a few more steps. The scary lady was close, but wasn't looking at Alice then. She was still making loud noises at her parents. Alice came closer to Simey. She remembered something. Simey had told her to do something. Yes, she was supposed to find Simey! Well, she had found him, now it was Simey's turn to find her. She touched him, then began moving away as fast as her little legs would carry her, smiling as she went, even though her legs didn't move as fast as her big Mommy and Daddy. Why did they have such large legs? Could she get some?

She looked back at Simey. But he was just staring at nothing. He hadn't moved. Why hadn't he come after her?

Maybe he wanted a toy to play with? Alice had the perfect idea. She pitter-pattered her way into Mommy and Daddy's room. There it was. One of Alice's favorite toys.

It was a shining gold object that went on fingers. Alice liked putting the thing on her fingers, it made her feel warm. Sometimes she could talk to people when she wore it. She liked it so much, she even tried to put it in her mouth once, but Mommy had stopped her for no reason. But now, it was on the small wood thing next to Mommy's bed that Mommy used to put her things at night.

She picked it up, and giggled as she felt the familiar warmth. Yes, Simey would like this toy.

She carried it back to the other room. The scary lady wasn't making any loud noises anymore, but her Mommy, Daddy, and the other nice man were still making loud noises. Much more noise than before. Alice didn't like it. Something told her she needed to get the toy to Simey fast.

She waddled over to Simey, nearly tripping as the

terrible sounds above her reached a high point. Was the scary lady hurting Mommy and Daddy?

Approaching the boy, Alice held out a hand with the shiny toy in it. Simey looked down, the first time Alice had seen him move.

"Foun' you." Alice smiled, and put the toy in his hand. He took it, turning it over, then put it on his finger. Alice put her little hands on his arm. "Foun' you," she said again. That seemed like the right thing to say.

Simey looked from the toy, to Alice, and back again. Then he looked at the scary lady.

"Get...her." Alice grinned and pointed.

~

KAT GASPED for air as the pain suddenly ceased. She was sure she had been about to die, for the second time. And this time, there would have been no coming back to full lucidity. She, Sergio, and Lance would have been a slave to Norma until the loop ended and they would die for real.

She wondered for a moment if she had died. All she could see for the first few moments were spots in her eyes. But as her vision cleared, she saw that they were still in the same room as before. But the red eyes of the huge ghost were fixed elsewhere.

Alice and Simon stood together. When had her daughter learned to stand without any help? Just how long had Kat been out of it? Simon was looking up at Norma's ghostly form, and he held something in his hand. A ring. The Argo Force ring! Where had he gotten his hands on that?

She looked at Alice, who had a sort of smug look on her

nearly two-year-old face. She pointed a finger at Norma. "Get...her."

"YOU MISERABLE WRETCH!" Norma swooped at Alice before Kat could do anything about it. She let out a soft scream as the monster hurled towards her baby daughter.

Norma stopped in mid-air, as if held by an invisible wall. And as Kat looked closer, she noticed a slight shimmer to indicate the barrier. She had seen that near-invisible wall before, in the Astral Plane.

Simon had his hand raised. He was still such a small boy, but to Kat's eyes right then, she thought she saw a glimpse of the man he would become. His eyes were resolute, and they had a wisdom seldom held by a boy his age. "Don't hurt them," he said to Norma. "I will hurt you."

"NO BOY, YOU NEED ME. WE NEED EACH OTHER TO SURVIVE."

"I don't need you. I have them." Simon gestured at Kat, Sergio, and Lance, all three of which were rooted to the spot. Simon slapped his hands together, and the action had a visible effect on the shimmering force field he projected. It fell inward, compressing.

"NOOOOoooo..." Norma's voice wavered and fell in volume as the wall fluctuated around her. Her spirit form coalesced, joining together until it looked solid, much like the woman Kat had first met, back when she was just a sickeningly-sweet real-estate agent. But this version of Norma was different. There were bags around her eyes, and her skin was a dull gray.

The bond was weakening. It was nearly gone. Kat hurried to Simon, putting her arms around him. "That's right, Simon. You have us. You don't need her anymore."

With each word, Simon stood up straighter, more confident, and Norma seemed to whither.

"What about all the fun times we had?" Norma's voice was almost a whimper now, and she lay on the floor, staring at Simon. "I was your mother."

A single tear dropped from Simon's eye. "My mother." And he wrapped his arms around Kat.

With a sigh, anticlimactic as it was, Norma fell apart. Her body disintegrated into a bunch of tiny pieces, which floated away until they too were no more.

Kat thought she heard screams from outside the house. Sergio ran to the window. "They're leaving," he said, a smile growing on his face. "All the ghosts outside, they're disappearing."

It appeared that the bond was broken. Simon turned to Kat. "Can you take me somewhere?"

"Uh, yes. Where do you need to go?"

"Old places. I need to stop the bad memories."

"You mean, like the tear in the foothills?"

Simon nodded.

"I'll get my car," said Lance.

They took Simon first to Norma's old house, the one where she had kept the boy against his will. Upon Simon's request, they lit a fire, and watched as the old house burned. One bad memory down.

Next, they arrived at the granary. This was where Simon's uncle had died, a source of great pain, and therefore a hotspot for the ghosts. They encountered no ghosts that they could see, but on arriving, Kat could swear that she heard the echoes of screams, as if from far away.

They burned that place as well, and Simon spent a while simply watching it burn, before putting forth his hands and doing something that Kat could not identify. Perhaps there was some residue of the ghosts here still, that Simon eliminated in the same way that he had eliminated Norma.

The park followed their trip to the granary. Simon didn't really do anything here, but the sun was coming out, and he and Alice laughed and played in the damp grass, while the adults watched. It was a joyful moment, and Kat let herself rest her head on Sergio's shoulder while they watched. They spent almost an hour like that, watching the kids play, then joining in themselves. Lance, in particular had a good time rolling in the grass and chasing Simon around. Alice tried to run, but fell over a number of times in her eagerness.

Finally, it was time for the last piece of unfinished business. They arrived at the foothills at dusk, not long before the time when the ghosts would appear.

Simon approached the place with a soberness that Kat wished no six-year-old boy should ever have.

"I was there." He pointed to the edge of the clearing. "She came to me there."

"Norma came to you there?" Kat asked. "So that's where all of this started."

Simon nodded. "I'm sorry. She hurt all of you."

Kat knelt down to his level. "Oh, don't feel bad, Simon. You didn't do anything wrong. She looked like your mother, and gave you something you needed in that moment. No one blames you."

Simon began to cry, and wrapped his arms around Kat. She hugged him back. "Let's close this breach and then maybe we can go out and get a milkshake or something. Would you like that?"

Simon nodded, a smile replacing the tears. Kat smiled too. "Yes? Well then, you've got this. Go show those ghosts who's the boss around here."

Simon straightened and turned to look at the space

where he had nearly died several years ago. "I can feel them. They want to come back."

"You're not going to let them, are you?" Kat said, encouragingly.

In answer, Simon put forth a hand, like he had to stop Norma. Something Kat did not understand, a will power, an intuition, somehow allowed him to interact with the supernatural here.

A thin line, invisible before now, began to glow with a strange light. A tear in the fabric of time and space. Kat recognized it as the same thin line they had seen from the other side, in the Astral Plane. It pulsed, responding to Simon's touch, and once again, Kat thought she could make out the faint screams of ghosts coming from within.

But as Simon faced down the tear, his arms outstretched, the line began to shorten. Where it had once stood at about the height of a man, it was now smaller, about Simon's height. Soon, it was nothing at all.

Simon breathed out as stillness took the clearing. And for the first time that night, they heard the sound of birds singing.

"You did it!" said Sergio, holding his hands out for a hug from Simon, who ran to Kat's husband with a look of delight on his face.

"Crumbs, boy, I think you just ended the cycle. Wouldn't be surprised if we could leave this place now, if we wanted."

"Yes, please," said Kat. The danger was past, but she didn't want to stay in this place any longer than she had to.

As they walked back to the house, they noticed people coming out of their houses, holding their heads and looking dazed. All of them were still here, still alive. Kat waved to a few neighbors she knew. They waved back, hesitantly, as if not fully realizing what was going on.

"This place has been reset for the last time," Lance said, staring around him. "They're all coming back."

They still had one problem, deciding what would happen to Simon. With everyone coming back to life, that probably meant that Trevor, Simon's uncle, would still be around. But given the way Trevor had treated Simon in the past, no one was too keen on letting him have custody again. Lance promised to come up with a few good excuses why he, Sergio, and Kat should take temporary custody of the boy, that he could use to explain the situation to the rest of the police.

Kat couldn't wait to test if they could leave the place, and sure enough, when they drove north of Greenfield, it wasn't long before they arrived in another town. It was the most beautiful sight Kat had ever seen. But they drove back to Greenfield in any case, until they could sort out what they would do next.

Kat looked forward to whatever the future brought.

EPILOGUE

"OH HEY! WE HAVE AN EPILOGUE THIS TIME!"

The High Matriarch of Earth stepped out of her quarters to see a number of her servants waiting. They knew she was not to be disturbed while she was in her personal quarters, and they had respected that command, as they should. But the moment the High Matriarch saw their faces, she knew that they were desperate to speak to her.

"What is it?"

"If it pleases your ladyship," said one of the young men attending her. He was pretty, that one. She should request his assistance more often. "The Vice President of Extradimensional Intelligence wishes to speak to you."

Ah, so that's why they were all eager to speak to her. Victoria, the VP of Extradimensional Intelligence was one of the High Matriarch's closest advisors, and she must really have some good news for her, if her servants were this on edge.

"Bring her to me in my waiting room." The young man bowed and ran to do as she requested.

The High Matriarch walked to the waiting room and

selected a few delicacies from another servant there, enjoying the sweet taste while she waited.

"My lady." A woman walked through the door and curtsied. "I have news."

"Good news I hope," she waved Victoria over to sit on the pillows beside her.

"Yes indeed, madame." Victoria reclined near the High Matriarch and accepted some of the food offered by the servant in waiting. "I believe I may have found the location of the girl, the baby girl, while she is still a weak child."

The High Matriarch sat up. "Alice? The Last Founder?"

"The very same, my lady. It seems, after the Founder Michael defeated our men in their dimension, he sent the girl and her family several decades in the past. We recently picked up a massive energy spike from a region in their version of California...from seventy years ago. We have no way of confirming that it was the child, but the signature matches what we picked up when Michael took out our men. It's worth taking a look."

The High Matriarch smiled. At last they had a lead to go on. They had seen nothing, no trace of the Rios family for months. Anything, even a vague clue like this one, was music to her ears.

"Send a team to investigate. I want that baby girl brought here."

"Yes, your grace. And what of the man?"

The High Matriarch knew to whom Victoria was referring: Sergio, their Sergio, the one she had originally sent to capture the girl. He had failed her, and she had punished him. He was still locked away in complete isolation.

"Forget him, he failed us before, he will fail us again if we let him. Send your best fighters and make sure some of my elite guard go with them." She wouldn't trust a group of men to get this job done for her, not without a few of her trusted warriors to accompany them.

"At once, my lady." Victoria stood and bowed before the High Matriarch waved her away. For the first time in over a year, she felt excitement build inside her. She would have that girl, if she had to tear all of Argo Force's precious Earth to do it.

She was the High Matriarch of Invergence after all. She always got what she wanted.

AUTHOR'S NOTE

Wow! So you not only picked up the free first volume in this series, but you actually read it and then decided you liked it enough to move on to the second one! That's incredible!

Ghosts of Greenfield takes our characters to a rather dramatically different setting than the first year, one set in the post-WWII past, and involving a number of ghosts. This is part of my endeavor to use this series as a kind of introduction to the many areas of my shared universe, in this case, the supernatural. Future volumes will explore other areas of the Argoverse.

By the way, apologies to anyone reading this who is from the actual Greenfield in California. I've never been there, so I may have made a few mistakes. I did a lot of research on its history and spent several hours traversing it in Google Maps, but I'm sure my account in this book is not perfect. Hopefully you don't get a bunch of tourists because of this book. Actually...scratch that. I'd love for these books to grow popular enough to fill your town with tourists! So here's to overrunning small towns with wide-eyed book nerds!

Thanks again for reading, and I hope you'll look forward

to my next book, where Alice, Sergio, and Kat will be taken on another adventure through time and meet some other heroes from...shall we say...another series of mine.

If you'd like to be notified of my new releases, special updates, bonus content, visit the website below to be added to the VIP Readers club:

VISIT JASONLEEHAMILTON.COM/SUBSCRIBE TO
JOIN THE VIP READERS CLUB!

If you want to keep up with me in the meantime, you can join the Argo Force Facebook Page, or follow me on Twitter and Instagram.

DID YOU ENJOY THIS BOOK? Please consider leaving a review on the site where you purchased it or on Goodreads— even if it's just a sentence or two. Every review makes a difference and helps other readers discover my books!

ABOUT THE AUTHOR

Jason Hamilton is an unapologetic nerd of all things science fiction and fantasy. He is the author of multiple fantasy series, as well as the Creative Director of the Arthurian Legends Universe.

The Site
www.jasonleehamilton.com

Facebook
facebook.com/argoverse

Twitter
twitter.com/storyhobbit

Instagram
instagram.com/storyhobbit

Patreon
patreon.com/jasonhamilton

Email
storyhobbit@gmail.com

ALSO BY JASON HAMILTON

Roots of Creation

A New Light (short story)

Out of Shadow

Growing Ripples

Through Fire

Into Storm

To World's Above

As Winter Spawns

Seeds of Hope

In Creation's Heart

The Faerie Queen

A King Revealed (short story)

Knight Rising

Knight Purged

Knight Spellbound

Knight Fallen

Knight Broken

Knight Awakened

www.ingramcontent.com/pod-product-compliance
Lightning Source LLC
Chambersburg PA
CBHW061213170626
46809CB00003B/1339